ABOUT THIS BOOK

Two women, one love, and a curse lurking in deep, dark waters.

For as long as she can remember, Maris Heilen has been haunted by dreams of a beautiful woman beckoning to her from beneath the water. These dreams have been Maris's only constant. She's lived her life like a leaf caught in the rushing tide: no rules, no commitments, and no long-term lovers, either—just a string of broken hearts that have tried to anchor her unwilling heart to the earth. When her dreams take on a new sense of urgency following the mysterious death of her estranged father, Maris knows it's time to uproot and keep moving, her soul pulled to the west, toward the water—toward *her*.

Instead Maris finds herself drawn to a surreal little town high in the Colorado mountains, where she begins to believe her dream might be much closer to reality than she'd ever imagined. When she discovers her past is linked to a legend even more haunting than her dreams—and that the woman in them is not only real but in danger of being lost to an unfathomable darkness—Maris resolves to outshine the evil that has crept into a small corner of a forgotten forest in Havenwood Falls.

HAVENWOOD FALLS BOOKS

Forget You Not by Kristie Cook

Old Wounds by Susan Burdorf

Fate, Love & Loyalty by E.J. Fechenda

The Winged & the Wicked by T.V. Hahn & Kristie Cook

Alpha's Queen by Lila Felix

Ink & Fire by R.K. Ryals

Lose You Not by Kristie Cook

Tragic Ink by Heather Hildenbrand

Nowhere to Hide by Belinda Boring

Flames Among the Frost by Amy Hale

Rock Me Gently by Susan Burdorf

From the Embers by Amy Miles

Defying Gravity by Kallie Ross

Break Me Not by Kristie Cook

How the Dead Lie by Stacey Rourke

The Lurkers Within by Danielle Bannister

The Collector: Awakening by Kristie Cook, R.K. Ryals, Belinda Boring & Nadirah Foxx

Addicted to You by Belinda Boring

Affliction Mine by C.J. Pinard

The Ward & the Wanderers by T.V. Hahn

Toil & Trouble by Melissa Wright

Of Salt and Stars by Seven Jane

Redefined by Morgan Wylie

Betrayal Among the Frost by Amy Hale

Forever Loyal by E.J. Fechenda

Fate's Demand by Emily Cyr

The Wu & the Wand by T.V. Hahn

A Demon's Redemption by JD Nelson

Also try the YA line, Havenwood Falls High; the historical paranormal line, Legends of Havenwood Falls; the darker, sexier side of town, Havenwood Falls Sin & Silk; and the local supernatural college, Sun & Moon Academy.

Stay up to date at www.HavenwoodFalls.com

ALSO BY SEVEN JANE

The Isle of Gold

OF SALT AND STARS

A HAVENWOOD FALLS NOVELLA

SEVEN JANE

To everyone who's ever fallen in love with the water.

And to MR, the brightest star in my sky.

The darkest hour is just before the dawn.
—Proverb

CHAPTER 1

MANY YEARS AGO

𝒶 t the edge of the lush green forests that surround Havenwood Falls, where the sweet-smelling junipers and majestic pines tickle the walls of the silver snowcapped mountains that border the town, in a place seldom traveled and even less often remembered, there once stood a well.

It was a well of the wishing sort, with a peaked cedar canopy that hovered above a yawning mouth of gray stone rendered soft by the breath of innumerable years. The well was one of those rare structures that during the day appeared carved of sunlight, its golden shine so blinding that the only way to look upon it was to shield one's eyes and sip it in quick glances lest it steal your vision completely. At night, however, the well was perhaps even more beautiful, when under the glow of a silver moon it seemed as soft and elusive as the stuff of dreams, formed into being by the twinkling of a thousand stars. Regardless of the time of day, the air always seemed more fragrant near the well—scented by day with a pomander of wildflowers and by night with the heady flora of thistle and night-blooming jasmine. So tangible, too, was the magic in this place that the air was always just a little cooler here—a wrap was necessary even during the hottest parts of the year—and it was so quiet that the whisper of the clear water that swelled nearly to the well's lips could even be heard above the rustling of the forest itself.

The animals that lived in the surrounding wood did not drink from the well, nor was its water harvested as drinking water for the town. Indeed, no bucket was ever hung from the awning from which to draw, for those few who knew of the well also knew that it was enchanted, and its waters imbued with a very special sort of magic. See, the well was not merely the fount of a spring. Far below the water's surface, in a hidden lake in a cavern below the earth, dwelled a creature as temporal and beautiful as the structure itself—a naiad by the name Noelani.

The naiad's well was a carefully guarded secret in Havenwood Falls, and only a few knew of its location, but those that were lucky enough to know the well's secret—most often women but occasionally men and children as well—would visit. There they would cut their hair and cast hushed wishes to Noelani, the Lady of the Water, and dip long wooden spoons into the well for a sip of her water's magic.

Most of the well's patrons—both human and supernatural alike—wished for love, for like other naiads, Noelani was a spirit of such things. Young girls were keen to look for their beloved's reflection hovering under the wildflower petals that floated on the well's surface. Older—but no less lovestruck—young brides garbed in their wedding dresses came to collect vials of Noelani's water, which brought them fertility. And when their bones began to ache, elderly women in their widow's habits sipped spoonsful of the well's water for vitality. If one was lucky, they might even catch a glimpse of the naiad herself, alight on the well's brim under the glow of the sun or the full moon, her long red hair swirling in the water beneath her as she sang songs more beautiful than those of the sirens at the banks of the waterfalls on the other side of Havenwood Falls. If this were the case, then the person would have been even more richly blessed, for it was said that whoever's eyes met Noelani's would be granted the gift of her magic, and some of her love would remain in their hearts forever, making all of their days blessed and sweet.

For many years, the naiad's well was a place of good fortune for all who visited. Noelani was happy, and her water was pure. But that was long ago, and such lovely places rarely endure for long—even those so consumed with love, for love is the most fickle of all beasts.

✦

The opposite of love is not hate but jealousy, and it was this that caused the well to ferment and the magic of Noelani to become diseased. It was jealousy of the ugliest kind—that which bleeds from the eyes and can sour milk just by the look of it—that led to the death of a young bride by the name of Stella Malley, who, on the very eve of her wedding, had come to ask the naiad's blessing and instead found herself drowned by the man who'd promised to marry her.

The manner in which he killed her—some say he held her head below the water until her lungs filled all the way to her throat, others that he strangled her with the train of her veil and sank her body with stones—is less important than his reason for doing so. The root of his this man's darkness was jealousy, not of what he couldn't have—for Stella had promised to be his—but of what he couldn't *control*. With her long black hair, creamed honey skin, and black eyes that sparkled like stars, Stella was as lovely as the midnight sky. But even more charming than her face was her heart, which drew others to her in droves and caused her to outshine the man who would have been her husband, and—had such a thing been possible—her shadow.

The man—his name important only because it is on the list of those that have been banished from Havenwood Falls, and such things are sparingly done—was a Mister Peter Heilen. And when Heilen forced his betrothed's face into the naiad's well, Noelani watched, helpless from below as Stella thrashed, the poor girl's lungs filling with water she could not breathe. As precious moments passed, Noelani saw the light inside Stella's eyes grow dim and faint until it burnt out altogether, and when the richness of her skin had been replaced with the gray tinge of death, her face relaxed and her mouth fell open.

Only Noelani heard Stella's final scream, and the sound was so anguished that when it infused the water, it also filled the naiad's heart with rage. With Stella's scream in her stomach, the naiad shrieked, her beautiful voice so racked with pain that when it broke forth from the water, the drops pierced Heilen's skin like shards of glass, causing him to stumble and look into the well. When he did, his eyes met Noelani's. He saw her red hair pooled like blood around her and her pearly white teeth grown long with fury, and he was afraid. And as the jealous are also often cowards, he ran, leaving Stella's body to topple into the well and sink, lost forever.

By the time Stella's corpse had made its way to the bottom of the well, it had turned the blue water black, and along with it, Noelani's heart. Death is a sorrowful thing, but murder is bitter, and crimes of passion are tinged with powerful dark magic that can snuff out even the brightest candle. Noelani's warmth turned cold as stone within her, and the love inside her drowned in a pool of darkness much in the same way that Stella Malley had been drowned in Heilen's.

Still, Noelani had seen the face of the man who'd murdered his bride, and so when he left the naiad's well, a part of her had been forced to go with him, trapped inside his eyes. The love held within Noelani's magic soon soured within him, turning every drop of love he encountered into something vapid and impenetrable until, one night many years later, he drowned in his bed where he slept—as dry and far from the water as he had been able to go to escape what he'd seen that night in the well. Heilen's death was a mystery, for how could a man as dry as a dead leaf choke on water that had risen up his throat from his own insides? But the doctors said he had drowned, and so he had. And because of the curse Heilen had brought upon himself and Noelani, there had been no one left behind to mourn his death, for he had never again had the chance for love.

✦

Time has changed the well. What was once a place of love and light has fallen largely to the ruin of legend. Years have passed since any girl or young bride or even a widow has dared visit its part of the forest, for they know there is no love left for the naiad to give. The well's once clear and flowing water has sunk lower and lower until all that remains at the bottom is salt from Noelani's tears. The cool air around the well has iced over, the remnants of Noelani's sobs still on the air in the form of ice and frost, and the forest has crept in around the well until the meadow has been overcome completely by a rambling snarl of thorn and root. The scent of wildflowers has been overrun by the stench of death, and in the absence of Noelani's light, the forest had grown thick with loveless creatures both cruel and vile.

None has seen the naiad Noelani, but those who tell tales of such things insist that Stella's bitter death consumed the once lovely creature, her beautiful red hair turned black, and her skin grew gaunt and pallid like a corpse left too long underwater. Those who might wander too far into the woods are warned to avoid the wrath of the well, for even if one were to survive the dangers of the forest, the creature that would crawl forth from her prison would not be the naiad, but a miserable and cursed thing. A rusalka they called Noelani now—a monster, dark and sinister, with a heart consumed with spiteful evil. And if she saw you, it would not be blessing that she'd give. Instead, she would pass on her curse and drag you down into the depths of darkness with her.

✦

The time of the well has passed, and the love of Noelani is lost. What remained of her magic passed to Heilen, and when he died, it faded with him—or so those who remember were inclined to believe. Noelani's story has faded largely to legend, and whatever remains of her—whether naiad or rusalka—is left to wallow in her well, guarded by the Court of the Sun and the Moon, who leave Noelani in peace so long as she brings no harm to the residents of Havenwood Falls. Some once whispered of a cure, a return of Noelani's love that could only be brought about from the seeds of her deepest hate, but it has been many years, and none have come forward that might break her curse and heal her broken heart.

And so Noelani waits, trapped in her own darkness, for a star to save her.

CHAPTER 2

*M*aris's eyes snapped open in the midnight darkness of her bedroom. She'd been having that dream again—the same one she'd been having her whole life. Okay, well, maybe not her *whole* life, but certainly for as many of her twenty-four years as she could remember. For the most part, they'd been the passing kind of nighttime fancies, the type that you woke up still feeling but only barely able to remember, and even those last little tendrils had faded completely by the time her feet touched the morning floor. But lately, the dreams had begun to linger, growing more and more insistent, as if they were trying to tell her something—to carve the memory of them into her heart with ghostly fingers and bedtime secrets. And they had begun to hurt, as if the longing in her dreams was enough to wound her heart, so that Maris sometimes woke with a dull ache in her chest.

Lately, her awakenings had grown even stranger. Sometimes she woke with her mouth full of warm, salty water. Other times she'd find strands of hair much darker than her own wound in the crevices of her body—around the backs of knees, her wrists, her throat—but when she'd go to remove them the strands would be gone. At first it had

7

baffled and confused her, and lately it began to frighten her, although it was impossible to say why because it was impossible to understand in the first place.

This bramble stuck in Maris's daytime thoughts, invading her dreams night after night in a pattern that had become as regular as her heartbeat. After Maris's father passed away a little more than a month ago—dried up and dead broke in some pitiful little hostel somewhere in the desert while she'd been buried under snow in Denver—the dreams had taken on an air of urgency, and the strange incidents had increased. Still, even though she often woke up sweat-drenched and panting, Maris could barely remember the dream by the time her eyes opened, and certainly couldn't recall enough to decipher any hidden message.

Insofar as she could tell, there was nothing truly remarkable about the dream itself. There was no grand inspiration or message that could be decoded with a dream dictionary, and she'd never once experienced any of that waking form of déjà vu that might connect the dream to her real life. The strange events aside, the dream wasn't scary or suspenseful—at least not enough that she would remember it being so. It wasn't even particularly thrilling. In fact, it was much the opposite. The scraps she could remember were beautiful—maybe *the* most beautiful she'd ever had, like something out of a fairy tale.

In the dream, it was always light out, but only just barely, with wisps of sunset coloring the sky in pastel shades of pink and orange. There was a forest she'd never set foot in and a small pool of water she'd never swum in, and both of these were more lush and vibrant than any parcel of land she'd ever seen—even in Colorado, where beautiful landscapes were a dime a dozen. But even more breathtaking than the scenery, there was *her*.

The woman in the dream.

The woman *of* her dreams.

The woman in Maris's dream was always constant, even if the scenery changed—which it did, but only with the weather, which followed the seasonal cycle of Maris's waking life. The woman—if she was that, because there was something distinctly magical about her

8

that marked her as not completely human but certainly feminine—swam in a large stone well. Sometimes the water that rippled atop the edges of the stones was frosted over with a layer of glittering ice; other times Maris could tell by its look that it was as warm as bathwater. Throughout all of these, however, the woman never changed. She always appeared, rising out of the water so that it spilled off her milk-white skin like rain and weighed down hair that was the color of liquid scarlet but might have been strawberry blond when dry. She had the most dazzling emerald-green eyes and a curve to her lips that was simultaneously taunting and coy, and she never wore anything more than a thin white slip of a dress, which gave her an air of innocence that was almost certainly misleading if one judged the way it clung, damp and revealing, against her flesh. She seemed always covered in dew and softness, and there was a small mark on the inside of one of her wrists: a tattoo of a star with four lines that stretched to create eight points—the one called the North Star.

"Maris," the woman would whisper, her lips shiny and wet with water and a voice that sounded like the ocean and deeper things and had a way of pulling Maris's heart into her throat.

"Yes," Maris would hear herself responding, as in her peripheral vision she watched her own hand reach for the water—for the woman in the water.

"Come away with me," the woman would say then, and the words were nectar on Maris's tongue when at last she closed the distance between the two of them and could taste the words on the woman's waiting lips. There was something that changed in Maris each time she kissed the woman in the well—a blossoming inside of her that grew and became more solid and real every time she touched the woman's lips with hers, until the dream had ceased to be a fantasy and began to feel like home.

If Maris had her way, she'd wrap every bit of herself—every strand of her dishwater blond hair, every square inch of the freckled, sun-kissed skin she'd inherited from the mother she'd never known, each of her ten long fingers and ten agile toes—around the woman in her dream. She'd hold her close, touch her lips against her sweet, glistening flesh, and slide with her beneath the water and never let her go. But then, just as this seemed like it might be a possibility, the dream would end, and Maris's eyes would open somewhere grim and dry and far away, the ethereal image of the woman's eyes tinting her vision emerald until she blinked it away. Darkness would creep in on the edges of the dream, and all would be lost—until the next night.

The woman in the dream had a way of undoing Maris, and not the least of it was because she was a *woman*.

Though she'd often been accused of being insatiable when it came to matters of the heart—a trait she'd had since puberty and had long since quit being ashamed of—Maris Heilen had never been terribly choosy about her lovers' genders. That wasn't to say she'd been particularly inclusive in her bedroom either, though whether that was by default or decision she wasn't sure. Honestly, the sex of her lovers had always paled in comparison to the actual act itself. Although her tastes had been diverse and far-ranging, her lovers had always and consistently been men. She'd bedded men with blond hair and with dark, men lean and bulky, those fair-skinned and those carved from ebony, tattooed and pierced and unadorned, smooth-faced and bearded, a decade older or a handful of years younger, and every possible combination in between. None had ever held her fancy for very long, though one summer she'd very nearly accidentally fallen for a Frenchman who'd had *chocolat* brown eyes and curling chestnut hair and who didn't speak a lick of English—something that had never been a problem for Maris when weighed against his gentle caresses and endlessly generous lovemaking.

In any case, no matter how many or how different the men that passed through Maris's bed, she was inevitably left unsatisfied, as if there was a hole deep inside of her that could never be filled, though she'd tried like hell to address that in the most literal of ways—not that she'd bothered herself to keep a tally of her conquests. A man wouldn't have done so, so why should she?

And through all of these men, Maris stayed empty, longing for something more that she could never quite articulate, let alone hold in her hands, until at last she'd come to believe it would never be a man who claimed her heart. Even so, Maris had never considered herself to be particularly attracted to women. But, if that was true, then so was the fact that she wasn't *not* attracted to women, either. They were beautiful and so lovely in ways that men just couldn't be, with their long smooth limbs and shapely curves, their soft blushing skin. It had simply never occurred to Maris to take one to bed, and she wasn't sure whether that was disinterest or some sort of deep insecurity—like if she finally opened herself up to someone she might fall into them, never to resurface. Lust, Maris was comfortable with. Lust she could control; she could embrace or let go and it wouldn't hurt her. Love was something else entirely. It was deep and bottomless, consuming.

To love someone, Maris feared, was to drown, and in that sea of emotions, she had never even learned how to swim.

Still, Maris couldn't deny that she felt something stirring within her whenever she caught herself looking at other women in the manner that she often caught men looking at her—all hungry-eyed and wet-lipped, like they were starving creatures just presented with a savory meal. Whatever it was that she felt, Maris had never done more than look, though no woman who had ever crossed Maris's line of sight could have compared to the woman in her dreams, including her *boyfriend*—a word Maris still wasn't entirely comfortable with two years into their relationship—who was currently asleep and snoring softly in the bed beside her.

Barely three months ago Maris had done something she thought she never would, not that she'd ever planned to find herself landlocked in Colorado to begin with. She'd agreed to relieve herself of her private little sanctuary in Lower Highland—a recent addition to Denver's neighborhoods known as one of *the* hippest new neighborhoods in the country—and shack up with a tech nerd from Capitol Hill. Not just any man, but Graham, her current long-term boyfriend who seemed to be becoming a little bit more serious about their relationship than Maris was totally equipped to deal with. Graham, with his unruly jet-black hair and rugged jawline. Graham, who knew how to wear a starched white dress shirt like it was lingerie, and often did, accessorizing his look with the top three buttons left undone under a shadow of dark stubble that had as much of a strange, weakening effect on Maris's knees now as it had on the first night they'd met. It had been the first thing she'd noticed about him when they crossed glances across the bar where she'd been slinging drinks for some extra cash: his unkempt hair and unshaven face juxtaposed against the stark white crispness of his shirt, a brooding counterfeit of a budding businessman. And Graham had not disappointed when Maris had given the last call and the pair had stumbled their way back between the sheets at her place.

Once upon a time, Maris would have taken Graham for a night, maybe two—three if the days bled together, which they often did—and then set him free to float away on the current of her spent desire. Such days, Maris reflected, seemed a lifetime ago now. Two years had a way of feeling like an eternity, and Maris wasn't entirely sure how she felt about anything so endlessly *long* and boringly predictable. She'd always been a free spirit, as restless as the tide itself, and now she felt stuck, like someone had built a dam around her heart and refused to set her free.

Maris's friends said she was settling for Graham, not because he wasn't handsome or stable or all the right things a man approaching thirty should be, but because he *was* handsome and stable and all the right things a man approaching thirty should be. And Maris would never admit it, but she knew she'd only settled for Graham. From his dark hair to his maddening tendency to root his feet in the ground and gather mud around them, Graham was unyielding and inflexible and aggravatingly *planted*. It was what had caused her to give Graham the nickname Grim, though she rarely called him that to his face. What Maris wanted—what she longed for—was the woman she'd been falling in love with in her dreams for the better part of two decades. She wanted to be *free*, as free as she felt in her dreams, where her ladylove waited for her.

Free like the water itself—fluid, flowing, and wavering.

"Come away with me," the woman in her dreams called, and Maris was desperate to go. This desire was bizarre and engrossing and endlessly frustrating, and the need to find this woman was so strong that it kept her constantly on her toes, afraid to settle and ever unsure of where to go. Maris was haunted by it.

But then, Maris had always been haunted, she reflected, her eyes staring at the expanse of ceiling above her head as she waited patiently to fall back asleep. Her father had, too, though he'd never spoken a word of it to his daughter. He hadn't had to. Maris could see it behind his eyes, a constant shadow of some unseen thing that waited for him just beyond the edges of his vision. She'd been able to assemble bits and pieces of his past, but much of the information was confusing and contradictory, like he himself was an unreliable witness. He spoke of a woman, whose face he couldn't remember, lost in a place he wasn't sure existed on any map, and he had insisted more than once these images followed him throughout his dreams in a series of nightmares that always ended with his own death. The last time they spoke, Maris confided her dreams to her father. In turn, he had warned her not to engage with the woman in the well, for it would only bring suffering on her, too. A week later, he died.

Maris's body must have reacted to the tense thoughts invading her mind, because next to her Graham's heavy arm slid reassuringly over her stomach, folding securely between her flesh and the mattress as he brought her body against his. It was an automatic gesture, and Maris allowed herself to be pulled into his gravity on the other side of the bed. She felt the tickle of his dark hair against her skin as he tucked his face into her neck and gently kissed her throat.

"Hey, babe," Graham murmured in a voice thick with sleep.

Something inside her stirred—a need to feel wanted, to feel loved —and the force of it only served to amplify the echoing hollowness in her chest.

"Go back to sleep," Maris whispered as softly as she could, smoothing away his hair.

Part of her wanted to wake Graham up, to pull the sheet away from his body so that the moonlight striped his bare chest and call him into her, but she didn't. With the woman's face still floating up in her memory, such a thing felt cheap and unfair. Instead, Maris let her body melt in the warmth Graham's kiss had left on her neck, hoping it would draw her back to sleep. She put her hand on top of his where it rested heavily against her stomach, forcing herself to reflect on the solidness of Graham's hard body around hers, his skin warm and inviting. It was too dark in the bedroom to see his arm where it lay across her body, but she knew from memory what it would look like— taut, tanned flesh against the stark white of the bed sheets. Graham was comfortable, and safe, but he was also an anchor, and the weight of him made it hard for Maris to breathe. She'd been with him for two years—longer than she'd been with anyone—and every day that passed had only made her sure of one thing.

It's time. The thought bubbled up from the bottom of Maris's thoughts and hung unspoken in the dark bedroom. Behind it came two more words, but these last were not Maris's. They belonged to the woman in the well, and they were sweet and sad and so full of longing that Maris felt a tear slip down her cheek as sleep finally reclaimed her.

"Find me," the woman was calling, and Maris was ready to go.

CHAPTER 3

*W*hen Maris next opened her eyes, the bedroom had filled with golden-yellow sunlight and Graham's side of the bed was empty. He had always been an early riser, usually up before the sun itself. This never bothered Maris. She enjoyed waking up alone—and as late as possible. Something about the night called to her, and she'd always found it difficult to sleep when the starlight was so bright overhead.

The condo was filled with the smell of freshly brewed coffee wafting in from the kitchen, and if Maris listened hard enough, she could hear the faint sounds of Graham flipping through the crisp pages of the *Denver Post* that was still delivered hot off the presses to their doorstep every morning, even though the world was already abuzz with digital news. A digital version of a daily paper simply did not meet Graham's standards. "Anything worth being considered news is worth being put into print," he was fond of saying, and she enjoyed chiding him for his antiquated ways, especially since he was a tech guru. But since Maris never bothered to read the news, it didn't really matter to her one way or another.

Maris slid out of the sheets and into the silk kimono robe that waited at the foot of her bed. She stepped lightly on the pads of her toes, trying not to make a sound as she glided across the hardwood floors toward the kitchen. As she'd expected, Graham sat at the breakfast table, shirtless with his back to her, the paper held in the air in front of him. Even while he was seated, Maris loved the way Graham looked from behind. Years spent in the gym had developed muscles in his shoulders and back she hadn't even known existed, and they bunched together and rippled apart as he brought the pages together and then reopened them. Somehow over the past two years, Maris had persuaded Graham to let his hair grow just a little bit longer, just enough so that his dark locks twisted into curls and she could tug at them between her fingers. On weekend mornings, if she could catch him before he'd combed them back, she could see the curls unkempt and tumbling down the back of his head to rest softly against the nape of his neck. This was how she found him now—his skin slipping smoothly into black drawstring pajama pants, his legs outstretched casually under the wooden dining table with his bare feet resting on the cold hardwood floor.

When she was near enough to touch him, Maris curled her arms around Graham's neck. Even with her doubts, it was impossible not to touch him.

"Good morning," she cooed, kissing his earlobe as she reached for his coffee. She liked hers with copious amounts of cream and at least two heaps of sugar, but Graham took his black. Maris held her breath and took a sip, ignoring the bitter sludge as a surge of caffeine sped through her veins.

Graham waited until she set the mug back down, then curled his fingers around Maris's hip and drew her into his lap with one arm behind her, fashioning a sort of hammock with his body so that she could lie easily in his arms. He tossed the paper on the table and brushed away a bit of hair that covered her face. "And good morning to you. How did you sleep?"

A quick image of her dream flashed in Maris's thoughts, and she answered around the blush that crept up her cheeks. "I always sleep well."

Graham smiled above her. It was patient if unconvincing. "Are you sure?"

"Of course I'm sure."

"Then I must have dreamed you woke up in the middle of the night again."

Maris didn't want to talk to Graham about her dreams. They were private. She'd only recently admitted that she'd been having more of them since her father's death, which Graham insisted was probably grief and a guilty conscience for not attending his funeral. Maris had told him plainly that her father hadn't left anyone but her behind to mourn him, and she could do that just fine from home, but although Graham listened and assured her he understood, she knew he didn't. She'd rather let him believe it was grief interrupting her sleep than have him know she was busy dreaming of another woman, waiting for her in a place that felt like home.

Realizing she'd not answered, Maris attempted to cover up her delay with a yawn. "I don't remember waking up, but maybe I did. No big deal either way, babe."

Maris had a long history with dishonesty, but she still hated to lie outright, especially to Graham. It didn't help that he seemed to have some sort of built-in lie detector—it had been one of the qualities that made his parents urge him to go to law school, a calling he'd rebuked, much to his family's dismay. He narrowed his eyes at her, but all he said was, "Well, good then. I'm glad you aren't bothered by those dreams anymore."

"Sleeping like a baby," she fibbed again, softening her lie with a shrug she knew would make the silk robe slip from her shoulder. When all else failed, distraction was an easy alternative—and Maris was something of a master at it.

Graham's dark eyes bored into hers and said quite plainly he didn't believe her. Then they flicked to the exposed bit of flesh that ran from her shoulder down to the curve of her left breast. Maris could feel her cheeks flush under the weight of his gaze as Graham's eyes softened and took on an entirely different emotion.

"I do believe you're blushing, Maris Heilen," Graham said, his voice dropping dangerously low and blossoming with heat. His jaw slackened, and his face took on the expression it always wore when he caught her coming out of the shower or undressing before bed, or singing in the kitchen while she prepared dinner, or working in the glow of her laptop late at night. Graham had a habit of having hungry eyes for her, no matter what she was doing, but then, so a lot of men had, over the years, and Maris had an equally large appetite. A thought crept into her mind—a remembered image of the woman in the well's shining wet lips—and the pink in Maris's cheeks deepened to red.

Maris was blushing, only not for the reasons Graham might have thought. But she bit her lower lip and played along, slipping into a fantasy that was much easier to wear than her true thoughts.

"Blushing? Oh no, I'm not blushing." She pretended to fan herself with her hand, waving it back and forth dramatically in front of her face. "It's just warm in here is all."

The sharp curve in Graham's raised eyebrow matched the smirk on his mouth. "It must be all the silk you're wearing," he said matter-of-factly, running his palm heavily down the front of her chest to let his fingers play at the folds of silk where they were belted across her waist. "Traps the body heat."

"This little old thing?" she teased, tickling his fingertips with the edges of hers. "Oh, I don't think it could be this little old thing causing this kind of *heat*."

As Maris purred the last word she could virtually see the thirst on Graham's lips as he bent his head back against the chair and inhaled deeply, the air shuddering around the lump in his throat. If she didn't know better, Maris would think he was a man trying to talk himself out of doing something impulsive, something he knew better than to do. But she did know better, and she knew he was just gathering himself to do exactly what he wanted.

With one arm still around her back, Graham laced his free arm under Maris's thighs and stood up abruptly, the chair clattering to the floor noisily behind him. He turned with her in his arms and began to walk solidly back to the bedroom, his eyes never leaving her face.

"Do you know what you do to me?" he asked in a thick voice. His hands were hot where they touched her skin.

"Yes," she answered, because she knew exactly what she was doing

—not talking about her dreams, or how desperately she needed to get away from her suffocatingly perfect life—and using Graham's desire for her to buy her some time.

✦

"There's something I've been meaning to ask you," Graham said, rolling over on his side to face her when they had finished their lovemaking. His hair was disheveled, and there were little beads of sweat running down the glistening perfection of his chest. Maris felt smug with satisfaction, and strangely empty too.

"What's that?" she asked, though she wasn't really listening. She was too busy idly tracing the tip of her finger down the sharp angle of his collarbone and feeling like she could answer any question he could dream up this time around. Maris never felt quite so powerful as she did after a nice romp in bed.

Graham pulled her wandering hand to his lips, brushed a quick kiss on her palm, and kept the tips of her fingers clasped in his hand as he rolled away. With his back momentarily to her, he produced a small jewelry box from the drawer of his bedside table. He returned, sliding closer, and gingerly placed the box down unopened on the sheets between them.

Maris immediately recognized the black velvet square, and an uncomfortable sensation coiled in the pit of her stomach. She'd noticed the box before, wedged in Graham's nightstand behind a stack of papers and other oddities men kept in their personal drawers, when she'd been looking for his spare keys a week before. Her sense of power deserted her, leaving her suddenly very aware of the lump that had risen in her throat, and very cold uncovered on the bed. Whatever question he'd planned to ask, Maris definitely hadn't been expecting this one. Worse, she knew the only answer she'd be able to give wasn't the one he'd be looking for, because no matter how she tried to sugarcoat it to save his feelings, it wasn't going be a *yes*.

Graham's pending question hung unspoken in the air between them while the box sat importantly on the bed. Maris stared at it and tried not to choke on her own breath. Beside her, Graham took a deep breath and stayed silent, tracing his thumb along the side of Maris's arm.

Under any other circumstance, Graham Parker was a man of bold gestures. He had doted on her unhesitatingly and lavishly, doing his damnedest to spoil her—to tame her with lavish gifts and promises of security, two things she'd never had, even when she'd asked him not to.

"Graham, we've talked about"—Maris waved her hand in the box's general direction—"this."

They *had* talked. Maris had made her feelings clear in a series of uncomfortable conversations, rebuttals of invitations to wedding showers, and complete aversion to anything that even smacked of marriage or babies or retirement planning. If Graham had listened at all, he'd have known this.

"I know it's a big step, Maris," Graham started at last, his words sounding tight and slightly stunted. He drew in another breath and held it until his body visibly relaxed. Then he opened the box's lid as he brought it and his body closer to her. Gently, he placed the box on top of Maris's chest, where it sat heavily atop her heart. The ring winked at her in the light of the bedroom, and in Maris's opinion, it had a distinctly mischievous look to it, like it knew what trouble it was stirring. It was beautiful, large, and faceted, and she hated it with every ounce of her being.

"It doesn't have to happen right away," Graham continued, and Maris realized she'd stopped listening and probably missed something —maybe missed *it*, the actual question. "But it's been two years, and I've never felt this way for another woman before. You've bespelled me, Maris, and I want to spend the rest of my life with you."

It was a sweet proposal, really, and as Maris finally dared her eyes to meet Graham's, she saw that it was also genuine. He truly loved her.

The poor dear. She never should have let it go this far. She should have walked away a long time ago—done what she always did best and take off long before things could get too serious and anyone could get hurt. No, that wasn't fair. They'd done this to each other, both her and Grim Graham. She'd stuck around when she knew she should have gone, and he'd tried to keep her when he should've known to let her go. Sure, the sex was great, but they could never make each other happy.

Graham opened his mouth, and Maris saw that dreaded question hanging on his lips, probably for the second time. She smiled at him as she closed the box and touched the back of her hand against the softness of his face.

"I'm sorry, Graham," she said, and she was, even though the vision of the woman's face was already floating up in her thoughts over his, filling her with the resolution that the time she had been waiting for had arrived—the very thing she'd been thinking since her eyes had opened in the darkness of their bedroom the night before. It was time to find the woman in the well. "I'm sorry, but I can't."

CHAPTER 4

*I*t took Maris longer to figure out where she was going than it did to pack up her belongings into the backseat of her midnight blue Toyota Rav4 and start trying to get there. By the time she'd loaded everything up, slid into the beige leather seat, pressed the button to start the engine, and thumbed through her Spotify playlists, Maris still wasn't sure exactly where she was headed, only that it was as far away from here—and from Graham—as possible.

To be fair, the whole process of leaving hadn't taken her long. Most of what she owned—namely, a few mismatched pieces of furniture she'd never liked anyway—she'd sold off when she moved in with Graham a few months back. The rest was mostly just clothes and other personal items, and even those were few. Now, even with all her worldly possessions piled in the back, her small SUV was full, but not overcrowded. Maris liked to travel light. Besides, she'd never been the sentimental type, not that she'd had much of that sort of thing to worry about holding on to—a side benefit of always being somewhere you were already planning on leaving eventually. A few carefully packed duffel bags and it was like she'd never been there. Now you see me . . .

Poof.

The biggest bump in her exit strategy had been Graham.

Honestly, the poor guy had taken Maris's refusal better than she'd imagined he would, not that he'd been particularly thrilled about it—not that she'd expected him to be. He hadn't yelled or raised his voice, and he hadn't broken down into tears, either. He'd just looked at her, confused and faintly disappointed, and—in a series of increasingly frustrated tones while he watched her pack up her things—asked her the one question she couldn't answer: *why*. He'd done his best to convince her to stay—he'd been working on that for their entire relationship, even though she'd told him not to and really should have seen this coming. Maris had thought up a litany of excuses—It's not you, it's me; I love you but I'm not *in* love with you; there's this woman I keep dreaming about—but eventually she just settled on *I'm sorry*. An apology wasn't worth much more than an excuse, but at least she hadn't had to lie to him. Again.

And so now she was sitting in her car, suddenly single and very much alone for the first time in more than two years, trying to figure out what the hell to do next. She didn't have a lot of prospects, but then she didn't have anything holding her back. The world was her oyster. She'd made it from Denver to Boulder, just far enough away from Graham's condo that she could breathe deeply again, and was idling in a Whole Foods parking lot at the intersection of the Denver Boulder Turnpike and Northwest Parkway, staring at the Flatirons in the distance and dreaming of water half a country away. Graham had called half a dozen times, each of the little incoming beeps grating on Maris's nerves until her lips had thinned to razor wire and she blocked his number—temporarily—just long enough for her to get far enough away that she couldn't feel guilty about not answering or going back. That was a lesson she'd learned the hard way: never turn around.

Keep going. Head for the water.

Maris thumbed open the navigator app, turned on location services, and slid her finger across the map on the screen of her iPhone. Colorado wasn't exactly a short distance from anything, but it was a central point to just about everything and all the water she could ever want—the Great Lakes, the coasts, the Gulf. East would take her—eventually—to the Atlantic. She could go south to Florida, or maybe north to New England, wind her way up the eastern seaboard. She'd always loved the leaves there in fall, though the Atlantic Ocean was browner than the Pacific and not clear enough for her taste. South would take her down toward the Gulf of Mexico, to New Orleans or Galveston Island, neither of which boasted particularly lovely waters. West was desert—her father's final resting place somewhere amongst those barren sands and saguaro cactus—but beyond that waited California and the Pacific Northwest and their white sands and craggy cliffs. North . . . no, she wouldn't go north. The only thing north was more land in every direction. She needed water, to be near the sea. She felt its call so strongly, it was almost as if her life depended on it, like she'd dry up and turn to dust like her father if she didn't go. She'd been landlocked for far too long.

And the woman, if she were waiting, would be near water. Even though she'd only seen the woman in the well, Maris knew this with a certainty that she couldn't question. If she could find the right water, she could find the well. She considered the compass rose on her map—a decoration on a digital interface—and considered the direction its needle pointed.

Despite her worries about finding herself in the desert, Maris turned her car west. Then she pulled back onto the turnpike as she twisted the volume knob on her radio to max and tried to remember the scent of saltwater.

✦

Four hours later, Maris pulled into a truck stop on the outer edges of Grand Junction to refill and reset as she watched the sky melt into a lovely shade of blushing strawberry orange that wasn't too different than the hair of the woman in her dream. Maris hadn't really thought farther than Grand Junction, and now that she was here she felt stuck, like she couldn't go any farther. She considered her map again and then, with a frustrated sigh, turned her phone off and tossed it in her backpack.

When Maris had packed up at Graham's, she'd done so the way

she'd practiced and perfected over a lifetime of rootlessness: the majority of her stuff was situated in the larger suitcases hidden under the privacy screen of her hatchback, and the important stuff and a few changes of clothes were neatly organized in her backpack in the passenger seat. This arrangement, Maris had learned, gave her endless options. Once, she'd done the same and ditched all of her stuff at a consignment shop on the side of the highway, sold her car at a used car lot, and hitchhiked all the way to Miami, where she'd gotten a gig aboard a cruise ship headed to the Caribbean. Another time, she'd left her car in an airport garage and sat on standby until she got a seat on a plane headed to Nevada just to see the Hoover Dam. As long as she had her backpack, she was golden.

It was the closest she'd ever come to feeling free, except for when she found a chance to swim, which, ironically, she rarely did. When she'd been little, her father had insisted the water would swallow her up whole like it had done her mother, who had drowned shortly after Maris had been born, in a swimming accident at the lake near where she'd grown up. Maris had often wondered if that's why her father had moved to the desert—to escape the water. She thought again of the simultaneous pull to water and fear of drowning, and wondered if she would share her mother's fate.

Feeling restless from her dark thoughts, Maris grabbed a bottle of water and a vegetarian cheese and pimento sandwich from the truck stop —she wasn't vegetarian per se, but had never been able to bring herself to eat meat from a gas station—and returned to her car, sitting inside the open hatch as she stared west. It was warm out, the sun was shining, and for the first time in a long time, there was a stirring in her heart. Part excitement and part anticipation, Maris felt as if she was waiting for something to happen. She had no idea what that might be, but she hoped it would be just the thing she was looking for. There was a small voice niggling in her innermost thoughts that teased her with the possibility that her dreams might soon be coming true in a very literal way—assuming such a thing was even possible.

Maris had just finished the first half of her cheese sandwich when she was ripped from her reverie by the noisy drumming of a shuttle pulling into the other end of the truck stop parking lot. Slowly, as if making its way directly toward her, it moved across the lot and headed in her direction. It was one of those big, fancy oversized buses, the kind that made road trips far more comfortable than they had any right to be. As it came to a stop a few feet away from her car, Maris saw the shuttle was wrapped in a banner that boasted stunning picturesque landscapes of a town she'd never heard of. Her eyes wandered through the scenes as she lifted the other half of her sandwich to her mouth. There were beautiful snowcapped mountains —something she'd frankly had her fill of, living in Colorado—rich, vibrant forests, and then, as the shuttle wheezed to a stop, Maris caught a glimpse of water.

It wasn't an ocean, and it wasn't the well in her dreams. It wasn't even a well, but a waterfall—the titular Havenwood Falls, Maris assumed—pouring down what must have been hundreds of feet to decant itself into a large pond that was surrounded by boulders at the base of the mountain. Still, there was something strikingly familiar about the water—the shape of it, which Maris could almost hear, cascading down the mountain, its waters clear and reflective even in photography. She'd never seen the falls, but it felt like the image of them was burned in her memory nonetheless, like an heirloom passed down through generations of Heilens before her. Through the picture Maris could hear the rushing sound it made; she could feel the gentle spray of the water as it splashed against the rocks that surrounded its base. Inside of these images, Maris smelled the water of her own dreams, floral and scented as if flower petals had bled out their fragrance within it. She could feel the cool dampness of it on her skin.

And the vision of the woman's face, fresh and wet and succulent, billowed up in Maris's thoughts. The woman smiled the distinctively coy smile that could only belong to her, and one of her fingers stretched out toward Maris, bending and beckoning as it played upon her heartstrings in the broad daylight of waking hours.

Maris forgot immediately about heading west.

She reached the bus before she even realized she'd started walking in its direction. The rest of her sandwich wasn't in her hand, and she had no idea what she'd done with it. She wiped her hands on her jeans, only half caring that it might leave a stain, and stared at the image on the shuttle's side. There wasn't much copy on the banner, just two words.

The name was inviting and mysterious at once. "Havenwood Falls," Maris read aloud, murmuring more to herself than to the driver, who saw fit to answer anyway.

"That's the place." He beamed as he stepped down from his seat and steadied himself on the pavement beside her. His eyes mirrored hers as they admired the waterfall on the banner together. There was an inflection in his voice Maris recognized but couldn't place, and for the first time in a long time, the telltale tingle of déjà vu pimpled her skin with goose flesh.

The driver was an older man, not quite elderly but well beyond the age that might be considered young, and the evidence of it showed in gray whiskers that decorated his face like Christmas tree tinsel. He had deep-set dark brown eyes and a complexion that might have been Hispanic or possibly Native American, and he was dressed head to toe in denim in a way that gave Maris the impression he'd be uncomfortable in anything else. He smiled at her, and it wasn't a stranger's smile but something much closer to one an old friend might give another that they hadn't seen in a while. "No other place quite like it."

Maris thought for a moment, reflecting on the various town names she'd seen on the app on her phone, and then said, "I've never heard of anywhere around here called Havenwood Falls. It wasn't on my map."

"Most haven't," the driver confirmed with a flick of his hand. A mischievous smile teased across his jowls as if he knew this fact and was proud of it—an odd thing for someone who drove a tourist shuttle. A curious thought moved through his eyes, and he studied Maris as she studied the image of the falls, his dark eyes turning shiny with interest as they flicked to her parked car and back. "Where you headed to, miss?"

Maris tore her eyes from the shuttle's wrapper and shrugged.

"West. Toward the ocean, I think. Just someplace . . . someplace else. Not here."

That was about the least specific answer—and the most accurate one—she could give, but the man nodded as if he understood exactly what she meant.

"Maybe Havenwood Falls is the place you've been looking for," he suggested. "Seems like you see something you like."

She wanted to object, but couldn't.

"The place is beautiful," she admitted, examining the banner again. "It looks . . . familiar." She wanted to add, "Like somewhere I've seen in my dreams," but didn't. That wasn't something a sane person said. Besides, Maris was positive she'd never heard of a place called Havenwood Falls before—not unless it was indeed the place she'd been visiting in her dreams, a thought that didn't do much to reassure her of her sanity.

This road trip was suddenly becoming complicated. Maris weighed her options. She could keep driving, ditch the car and hitchhike, or find an airport and an open seat on a plane to somewhere. The strawberry sky was quickly running to hues of deepening purple, even though it was barely six o'clock—an early night for early spring. Whatever she did, it would be night soon, and she'd need a place to camp out. A rude little thought reminded her that it would be the first night she hadn't sleep beside Graham in more nights than she could count. She didn't care about that so much, but she wasn't particularly looking forward to sleeping alone. An empty bed was a cold bed. Maybe she'd meet someone in Havenwood Falls.

"How far is it?" Maris asked, dismissing the thought almost as quickly as she had time to think it. To hell with Grim Graham and his proposal and his boring life, and to hell with feeling lonely, too. "I've been driving for a while. Maybe if it's close, I'll stay a night before I keep going."

The driver sucked his teeth thoughtfully, eyeing Maris's well-packed SUV a few steps away. "Well," he said, "it's not that far. Just up the mountains a ways."

Maris nodded as if she'd made up her mind. She *had*, but she hadn't exactly meant to. She'd meant to go west, toward the ocean, not up, higher into the Colorado mountains and some strange little town she'd never heard of—but what good was fleeing a perfectly boring life if you didn't recolor it with adventure?

"Perfect," she decided. "I'll follow you whenever you're ready to head out. I just need to fill up."

The man smiled, but it was shallow. "Roads are tricky up that way. If you don't know where you're going, it's real easy to get turned around—maybe miss a turn and end up on the other side of nowhere up in the mountains. Why don't you climb aboard? I'd be happy to give you a lift. No charge."

Maris considered this. She'd never liked driving up those windy mountain roads.

"If you're worried about leaving your car here, don't be," her would-be driver added, as if reading her thoughts. "The town's got an agreement with this stop, knows visitors up to Havenwood Falls leave their cars here and take the shuttle up. Town's not that big anyway, easy enough to get around on foot. If you decide to stay, there's a service that'll tow it up for cheap."

Maris didn't need any more convincing. The violet sky was quickly darkening into eggplant, and the thought of a secluded little getaway was relieving anxiety she hadn't known she had. "Okay," she agreed. "I'll grab my bag. Are you waiting on any other passengers?"

"Looks like you're it. All aboard."

Under normal circumstances, Maris might have been skeptical—hopping onto a bus to a place she'd never heard of with no other passengers and a driver who seemed keen on being mysterious. Today, she just felt lucky. As she retrieved her backpack from her car and locked everything up, her eyes found their way back to the wrapper on the shuttle, to the falls flowing freely down the side of a sparkling mountain, and she closed her eyes and thought about the woman in the water.

West could wait. Tonight she was going to find the water in Havenwood Falls—and whatever waited for her there.

CHAPTER 5

*P*urple had bled to black and the stars were in full view when Maris opened her eyes again in her seat at the back of the shuttle. She hadn't felt tired when she'd boarded the bus in Grand Junction, but that was kind of beside the point now, since she was peeling her face from the fabric of her backpack, which had been repurposed as a makeshift pillow. She hadn't slept much last night and so must have been lulled to sleep by the steady turning of the tires on sparingly traveled roads under a darkening sky. The last thing Maris remembered was rolling across the truck stop parking lot back in Grand Junction, watching her SUV shrinking to a small dot as the bus rumbled onto the road that led up into the mountains. Either she'd fallen asleep before they'd ever made it fully back onto the highway, or they'd made their journey up the mountain in the space of a single blink.

It didn't much matter now—not that Maris cared. Sometimes part of the adventure was the journey there, and following her heart and hopping on board a shuttle on a whim at a truck stop certainly counted as adventurous, spontaneous, and impulsive—all things her father and her newly *ex*-boyfriend had never appreciated about her. Even though she was half asleep, the thought managed to lift Maris's lips into the closest thing she could manage to a smirk. She loved moving about life like a piece of wreckage caught in a storm, taken wherever the tide fancied carrying her. At the moment, however, she was anxious to get off the shuttle and stretch her legs—and her neck. The backpack had left an unpleasant twinge in her shoulder. They had to be nearly there anyway; the driver had said it wasn't a long way.

She was just about to ask, when, sensing she was awake, her driver called out to her over his shoulder. As his voice carried, his eyes met hers in the rearview mirror. "Well, hello again," he said cheerfully—a mite too cheerfully to the ears of someone still stuck in the cloud of half-sleep. Still, the sound of his voice gave life to the quiet of the bus and Maris along with it. "We're just about to our destination. Not much longer than a few minutes now and you'll be getting the best view in Havenwood Falls. Taking you right to the top." He emphasized this last with a good-natured wink in the rearview mirror and a haughtily pointed index finger raised to the underside of the shuttle's roof.

Maris nodded and stretched, trying not to groan as she worked the kinks from her sleepy limbs, which were more sluggish than normal. When she yawned, her breath caught in her throat. Everything felt dry. Her breath was shallow, and her stomach was uneasy. Altitude sickness was kicking in. She had no idea how high they'd climbed, but it was enough that she was feeling the impact of it. Peering out the window, all Maris could make out in the darkness were the fuzzy, shadowed shapes of rocks and trees and other such things you'd expect to see in the Colorado mountains.

"Sorry to fall asleep on you," Maris said, when her brain fog had cleared enough to allow speech. The words came out slurred on parched lips. She cleared her throat and tried again as she dug around in her bag for the bottle of water she'd brought with her. "Doesn't make for a fun passenger."

"Oh, not a problem. It's a nice ride to relax. I'd probably take myself a nap too if I weren't the one driving." He followed this with a chuckle that made Maris laugh despite the fact that he hadn't really said anything funny.

Maris was still struggling to wake up. Her nap had been that heavy kind that daytime dozes often were—heavy and lingering, the kind that left one feeling groggy and far more tired than they had been before they ever fell asleep. Blinking the sleep from her eyes, she extracted a tube of lip balm from her pocket and rubbed it against her mouth, enjoying the minty sensation that hydrated the desert that had formed on her lips. She rubbed at her cheeks to bring some sensation back to her skin and then attempted to smooth her hair, which the dry mountain air had spun into a static spider web. She was technically awake, but not quite awake enough for her body to realize it yet. Numbness clung to her bones and everything had a hazy quality to it, as if she were stuck in that place between sleep and waking. It wasn't a bad feeling, particularly after the events of that morning. A few hours ago, she'd woken up in a life she had never felt comfortable in, and now she was half a state away, on a shuttle at night in the middle of nowhere with nothing but a backpack and—Maris checked her pockets—a mostly dead cell phone that currently had no signal.

Most people might have been unnerved, but to Maris, it was invigorating. She was loving every minute of her new adventure. Briefly, she considered unblocking Graham's number, but then decided against it.

A few minutes later, feeling had finally returned to Maris's limbs as the shuttle crept up a long gravel driveway and bumped to a stop. As the driver slid the door open Maris could hear the roaring sound of rushing water in the distance, and she let the noise play in her ears as he came around the side of the shuttle, opened the door, and extended his hand. Maris accepted the driver's outstretched hand, and the scent of fresh water rose around her as she stepped down onto the pavement. Even in the dark, she could just make out the fine mist rising over the edge of the falls. She didn't know anything about Havenwood Falls, but she knew where he had brought her.

"It's the falls," she mused to no one in particular, slinging her backpack over her shoulder in preparation to make her way to see them.

Her driver released his grip on her hand and, steering her away from the falls, gestured grandly toward a large building that waited at its top. "Figured you might be hungry when you woke up, and I noticed the way you were looking at the falls, so I thought this was the first place you should see."

As he said it, Maris's stomach rumbled. "Definitely," she agreed. "Thanks."

The driver clamped a fatherly hand on her shoulder. Normally Maris would have hated such a gesture, but this one felt kind of nice. Warm and reassuring. Friendly.

"Enjoy your time at the falls," he said by way of goodbye, and Maris could hear the capital letter, marking the import of the statement.

Maris took a deep breath and inhaled as much of the scent of water she could. It wasn't exactly the scent she'd been craving, but it was close enough.

"I plan to," she said.

✦

Fallview Tavern & Grille presided over the crashing water with all the dignity one would expect from what was clearly a landmark building of obvious significance. It was either authentically old or the architect who had designed it had done a spectacular job of emulating a nineteenth-century log-sided tavern with all the proper trimmings. There were some modern twists as well, designed to embellish the natural beauty of the falls, which were spectacular on their own. Just around the back of the tavern, illuminated by the glow of fairy lights, a multilevel patio was webbed with staircases. The lights' eager twinkling gave the impression that the tavern was a live, moving thing and not a simple building.

As much as she wanted to explore the widow's walk that overlooked where the falls slid off the mountain, Maris's stomach was calling. Obeying the demands of her appetite, Maris made her way to the wide entry doors and stepped inside the tavern, allowing the beautiful rustic behemoth to swallow her whole.

As impressive as the outside was, the tavern's inside was even grander, and when Maris's breath caught in her throat again, it had nothing to do with dryness. The interior was large and spacious, with high ceilings held aloft by wooden support beams that wore a large iron chandelier like an earring. A large stone fireplace rose above hardwood floors that may have been original, and the walls were lined with iron sconces. Each was situated with thick candles that added flickering glows that danced along the edges of the space, reflecting from skylights that undoubtedly flooded the room with sunshine during daylight hours. Tables and chairs were scattered about the large dining area, giving the space the sort of carefully orchestrated haphazard look that people paid a lot of money to fake. All of the tables were currently empty, and many had their chairs overturned on their tops, a sure sign that closing time was drawing near. Tasteful and artistic with a rugged-meets-modern sort of vibe, the tavern was the perfect blend of the old world and new that was so smooth and seamless, it seemed almost crafted by magic, and Maris—who had always held an appreciation for architecture—instantly fell in love with the place.

"Hello there," called a man's voice from the bar at the back of the room. Maris had long ago learned how to assign faces to names purely from the sound of their voice, and she had an uncannily accurate knack for it. The owner of this voice sounded young, masculine, and decidedly handsome—not that Maris was interested; it was just the sort of thing she noticed. Swiveling toward the bar, Maris approached the black marble surface and the man who stood behind it. A dishrag in hand, he wiped dry a glass with the expert flourish of someone who knew his way around a restaurant and was proud of it.

Maris had been right in her assessment of his voice. The man behind the bar was probably not much older than she was. He was of lean build—the kind people called a swimmer's body—with curly brown hair and blue eyes that added the only real dash of color to the room. He was dressed simply in blue jeans and a black V-neck T-shirt, and she could see the edges of a tattoo that climbed up the expanse of what appeared to be a rather hairless chest. It was hard to tell what it was, but it looked tribal—maybe a dragon, or some other type of winged animal.

As Maris approached the bar, the man set down the glass on the counter and extended a hand. She expected him to tell her that the place was closing, but this was before she noticed the way he looked at her—more or less that same double-take most men did when they first saw her, but his glance was a little more knowing, like he thought he'd seen her somewhere before, though of course he hadn't.

Rather than updating her on closing time as she'd expected, he said instead, "Welcome to Havenwood Falls and Fallview Tavern. You must be new in town." It didn't sound like a question, but Maris nodded anyway. "Name's Simon," he continued. "What's yours?"

Maris accepted his hand and returned what she hoped was a confident shake.

"Maris. Maris Heilen," she said. She thought she saw something shimmer in Simon's eyes when he heard her name—some confirmation of that recognizing look from before—but she assumed it was a trick of the flickering candlelight. It was impossible that anyone here would recognize her name, so she ignored it. "How did you know I was new in town?"

Simon flipped the towel over his shoulder and shrugged. "It's a small town. New faces stand out, and only folks riding in on a shuttle show up this time of night."

"Yeah, right. It dropped me off right outside." She looked around at the empty restaurant. "You own this place?"

"Nah," he said. "Just the cook. Speaking of which, what can I get you? On the house."

Maris felt her eyebrows pull upward in suspicion, and she softened this with a coy smile and a tilt of her head that showed off the smooth curve of her cheekbone. She leaned forward on the counter so that her breasts pressed beneath her thin camisole. This were largely automatic, a posture she'd practiced often when preening for tips on the other side of the bar. "On the house?"

His smile matched hers. "Sure. First night in town deserves a welcome meal."

"How about a first night drink?" Maris wasn't trying to flirt, but Simon was too cute to resist, and she enjoyed having people in her gravity too much to ignore the opportunity.

Simon laughed and might have blushed a little. "I'm happy to grab you a beer, but I'm afraid I'm not much of a bartender. Anything I mix up is likely to taste like bilge water."

It was Maris's turn to laugh. "Well, we're in luck. That's my specialty."

"Bilge water?" Simon winked.

Maris laughed again, feeling strangely happy for the first time that day. Like the shuttle driver, Simon felt more like an old friend than a shiny new stranger. "No, not *bilge water*—bartending. I'm a bartender by trade"—a brief glimpse of the life she'd left behind passed before her eyes—"or at least I used to be, in my last life."

"Last life?" Simon was humoring her. There was that shimmer again in his pale blue eyes as he pulled a glass from under the counter and pushed it toward her, then motioned she should come around the bar. She did, trying to name the color of his eyes as she moved. Blue— they were definitely blue—but there was an interesting sort of iridescence about them, as if they were scales instead of eyes, refracting the light in little prisms. Reptilian, but not cold. When she looked closely, Maris half expected a second inner lid to slide over and wet the eye. Whatever it was that made them sparkle like that, it wasn't scary— but it was damned sexy. She'd never seen eyes like his before.

Again, not that Maris was interested. It was just hard not to appreciate.

"I reincarnated today." Maris grinned over her shoulder at Mr. Sexy Eyes as she plucked a few choice bottles from the liquor rack behind the bar, selected some juices from the mini-fridge beneath the bar top, and scooped three ice cubes into a cocktail shaker. "Left my old life and decided to start a new one. Happened across a shuttle here while I was taking a rest in Grand Junction, and, well"—she made a motion with her hands like a stage magician might before a particularly stunning trick—"surprise. Here I am."

Turning her eyes to her work, she began mixing various liquors together in the shaker without bothering to measure amounts, then poured the mixture into a wide-rimmed martini glass. Finished, she grabbed a peeling knife lying nearby and curled off a piece of lemon zest for garnish. Then she lifted the glass and, with a flourish, handed it to Simon.

"Deep blue sea martini. Family recipe." She beamed. "And my signature cocktail."

He sipped, and the pleasure in his mouth rippled across his features. "This is delicious."

"I know."

Simon took another long swallow, licked his lips appreciatively, and settled the mostly empty martini glass on the bar top as Maris mixed one for herself. "So, how long do you plan on staying in Havenwood Falls?"

Maris considered. Timelines were never her specialty, and she was a horrible planner. She hadn't meant to get here, but now that she was, there was nothing inside of her that compelled her to make a hasty exit. Quite the opposite, in fact: she'd barely seen anything of this quiet little town, but it felt like . . . like she belonged here. It felt like she was meant to find this place. And somehow it was all connected to the woman in the water—the woman in her dreams. Maybe it was destiny, or some weird trick of fate.

Of course, that was not something she was going to share with her handsome new friend, who was currently letting his sexy blue eyes wander all over her body. She shrugged. "Might stick around for a while, assuming I can find a place to stay and a way to earn my keep."

"Well, the best place to shack up around here is Whisper Falls Inn. Right down in the heart of the town square, but if you listen real hard, you can still hear the falls. I can call a Luber for you—it'll take you right down there and get you settled in. I hear the rooms are . . . cozy."

As he talked, Simon moved closer to her, until Maris could feel the heat pulsing off his body and reflecting back against hers. She inhaled, and his scent was musky and intoxicating—primal, animalistic even. When Maris lifted her head to look at him, it was through half-lidded eyes. "Well, I'm halfway to staying a little longer then."

She was tempted to reach out to stroke the side of his face, but his fingers were already on her hand. She inhaled sharply as he took the glass she'd forgotten she'd been holding and lifted it to his lips, smiling. Maris laughed breathily and tucked a stray strand of her dishwater blond hair behind her ear, trying to recalibrate.

She was about to say something—probably some innuendo about the cozy cottages at Whisper Falls Inn—when he spoke again. "In regards to earning your keep," Simon went on, his voice dropping to a throaty sort of teasing tenor that toed the line between business and pleasure, "if this is how you mix drinks, I think we can find a place for you behind our bar."

Maris forgot all about flirting and swallowed back her witty repartee. "Really? You'd give me a job?"

There was a sharp noise behind them, and Simon spoke without tearing his strange iridescent eyes from Maris. His voice was normal again, but his body heat was still on high. "Isn't that right, Odette? We've been looking for a new bartender. Seems one might have found her way to us."

Maris spun on her heel to see a handsome woman standing behind them, positioned almost perfectly beneath the large iron chandelier that hung in the center of the room as if she'd walked in through the patio doors from the falls outside and been pinned there beneath a giant magnet. She was tall and shapely and could only be described as elegant, possessed of a beauty that made her seem somehow ageless, and possibly too beautiful to be completely of good intentions. There was a waiting dark lurking behind her pale skin and delicate yet severe jaw structure.

Something in Maris quickened as she stared at the woman who walked toward the bar, her eyes never leaving where they had speared into Maris's. She watched Odette approach, and Maris had the distinct feeling that air was being sucked from the room. Still, there was something alluring and recognizable about the woman, and Maris saw the woman in the well in the way the other woman's limbs moved, as if she were swimming rather than walking, treading water with her footsteps.

When she was a few feet from the bar, Odette's eyes left Maris and moved to Simon, who introduced everyone in a voice straining to sound casual. "Odette, this is Maris Heilen." A flash of recognition moved in Odette's eyes, a similar flicker to the one Maris had first seen in Simon's when she'd given him her name. "She's just arrived in Havenwood Falls. Maris, this is Odette Alverson, owner of Fallview."

"Nice to meet you," Maris managed to say, but Odette's expression remained unchanged.

For a moment, the tavern's proprietress said nothing, but then she smiled, and it had the effect of changing her face completely, reshaping it from something mildly terrifying and spectral to a warmer, softer, much more human expression.

"Nice to meet you, Maris Heilen. Yes, I do believe you'll be an excellent addition to our little family here at Fallview Tavern." She cast a meaningful look at Simon and then back at Maris, who knew a dismissal when she saw it. "At the moment, though, we're just about to close. I've sent for a car to take you over to Whisper Falls Inn. You can start tomorrow," Odette finished. Maris shot a look at Simon before retrieving her backpack from the patron side of the bar.

The temperature in the room had gone from warm to cold, chilled but not unwelcoming. It was a little enticing actually, like slipping your toes into pool water for the first time.

"Great," Maris smiled, biting her lips to stymie the excitement she felt bubbling in her veins. "Thank you both. I really appreciate it. See you tomorrow."

With a wave goodbye, Maris made her way out of the tavern to the single car that was sitting outside, engine running. She did a double take. She'd expected Uber—assuming she'd misheard Simon earlier— or even the traditional yellow cab. Maybe some local car service if the main ride-sharing service hadn't made it out this far. Whatever this ride was, what was waiting for her wasn't anything she might have expected. The car was orange and old, and Maris was pretty sure it was a hearse and not a town car. It flashed its headlights at her, and she walked toward it.

Taking a last look over her shoulder at the tavern, Maris watched as Simon and Odette moved together and stood side by side in the large picture window. Simon lifted his arm in a friendly wave goodbye as Odette's sharp eyes stared out across the darkness, her expression haunted and far away.

Maris's eyes must have been playing tricks on her, but as she stared at the figures watching her, she thought she could read the words moving across Simon's lips.

"You know who she is," he seemed to say to the woman beside him, and to this Odette's lips moved in a statement equally as odd.

"Worse," Maris thought she read Odette Alverson say, "I know *what* she is."

CHAPTER 6

*M*aris was starting to believe everything in Havenwood Falls, people included, must have belonged to another time, or another place, or otherwise be made of a substance slightly different—and much more interesting—than what passed for normal in the rest of the world. Everything here seemed vaguely surreal and just a little abnormal—not anything that anyone who wasn't looking for it would notice, but enough that Maris, who had always enjoyed people-watching, was starting to pick up on. The people she'd met so far, including the fatherly shuttle driver (whose name she never caught), Simon with his iridescent blue eyes, Odette Alverson and her strange beauty, and now her Luber driver—a funny little man called Jakeel who sported a thick mustache and a disco shirt and was so small he'd added a child's booster seat to help him see over the steering wheel of his car—were all just a little more colorful than your average person, and even in the dark, Havenwood Falls was just a little too picturesque to be real. It was a postcard come to life, and there was a constant tinge of enigma in the air that tickled along Maris's desire to know more.

Whisper Falls Inn, Maris soon came to find as she rolled her window down to get a better look, was no different. She watched as the large, three-story Victorian appeared in the headlights of Jakeel's bright orange Luber née hearse. Positioned diagonally on the corner of two streets, right in the southeast corner of the town square, as Simon had said it would be, the place was larger than life. It sat somewhat haughtily, sandwiched between parking lots and surrounded by a privacy tree line. And, even though it already amassed more than half of a city block, it still seemed hungry for more.

True to its architectural heritage, the inn had all the trimmings of a proper Victorian: a wraparound porch, turrets, bay windows, and a swirling gingerbread trim. It was hard to guess how many guest rooms might be in the home, but Maris had to assume they were numerous. There was an expanse of lawn that connected the main house to a line of cottages, and although the property had the authentic look of one that might have dated back to the previous century, it was obviously well cared for.

"Here we are," Jakeel announced, though it really wasn't necessary, as the car crunched to a stop in front of the main entrance. "Whisper Falls Inn. Family run and operated for just about as long as the town's been around. Michaela Petran runs it now—nice girl, probably close to your age—you'll probably find her waiting for you inside."

Maris slung her backpack over her shoulder and leaned forward to pay her driver. He waved her hand away and wriggled his mustache at her instead. "No way, honey," he said, eyes sparkling mischievously. "Your new friends over at Fallview already paid the tab."

Maris blinked. Well, that was a first. "Seriously? Well . . . that was really nice of them."

"Most people here in Havenwood Falls are nice enough, unless you find yourself on their bad side." He winked to soften a statement that Maris suspected had a lot of truth hidden in it. Then he gave her a look that bordered on dangerous, but not particularly unpleasant—a totally weird combo. "Plus, it's good to have fresh blood in town."

It wasn't very often that Maris found herself lost for words, but right now was one of those moments. The vibe she felt—the one that suggested there was more to Havenwood Falls than might meet the eye —was so strong it was strumming her insides like a bass violin. "Okay," she finally managed as she opened the door and swung one leg into the night air. "See ya."

Jakeel's eyes were already back on the steering wheel. "Yep, see you tomorrow."

"Tomorrow?"

She could see a smile creep up the side of his face, pushing his thick mustache upward like a caterpillar moving up a branch. "I'm the only driver in town, honey, and you ain't got no wheels."

Oh, right. Maris hadn't really thought about that, not that she ever worried about moving around, car or no car. "That's true," she agreed as she shut the door behind her, having no idea *when* she'd actually see the odd little man again but figuring she very likely would. "See you tomorrow then, Jakeel."

"Night, Ms. Heilen," Jakeel returned, sending a wink over his shoulder with one eye before both made their way to the house waiting at Maris's back through the still-open backseat window. "And don't let the bedbugs bite."

With a little bit more acceleration than was entirely necessary, Jakeel sped away before Maris could remember ever telling the odd little man her last name.

✦

The woman named Michaela Petran—who did indeed appear to be around the same age as Maris—was, as Jakeel had suggested she'd be, waiting for Maris behind the front counter of Whisper Falls Inn. She was a few inches shorter than Maris, with dark brown hair and the most beautiful gray-green eyes that Maris had ever seen. Or perhaps they were the *only* eyes that shade of gray-green that Maris had ever seen. The folks in this town either had some wicked eye pigment genes or one hell of a contact lens supplier.

"Hey," Maris said as she dropped her bag at the counter and began rummaging around in its pockets for her wallet. Finding it, she handed Michaela her credit card and ID. "I'm looking for a room, or maybe more than a room, I guess. Don't know exactly how long I'll be in town."

"You're Maris Heilen?" Michaela confirmed in a friendly but

decidedly no-bullshit kind of way without actually looking at the cards in her hand. When Maris didn't answer immediately, Michaela added an explanation. "Got a call from Simon up at Fallview that he was sending a visitor down by way of Jakeel. We get a lot of late-night arrivals."

"Oh," Maris breathed out, pulling her phone automatically from her pocket to check the time on the screen. It had died, its poor little twelve percent of battery life apparently not enough to keep it ticking till she could find a place to recharge. Then, worried that Michaela's hesitation might be the result of a space issue—it had never occurred to her that maybe there'd be no room at the inn—Maris leaned forward, biting on her lower lip as was her habit when she was nervous. "Please tell me you have a room? I don't get the feeling there's a Marriott around the corner for visitor overflow."

Michaela laughed and returned Maris's cards to her in addition to a large brass key. "Yes, we have room. Believe it or not, it's the slow season." Maris took the key as Michaela explained how to get to her room. "The cottages are mostly full, though, primarily with family, and it can be a bit noisy at times with all the coming and going. I'm putting you upstairs, in one of the luxury suites in the third-floor turret. Figured it might be nice for you to be in the main house, and it's one of the only places in the house to catch a glimpse of the falls— that okay?"

It was Maris's turn to laugh. "A suite in a turret? I'll take it. Sounds like something out of a fairy tale"—Maris considered—"or a dream."

The smile Michaela gave Maris now reminded her distinctly of similar ones she'd seen on Simon's face, on Odette Alverson's, and even on Jakeel's. "You look like the kind of girl who likes to dream."

Maris didn't know what that meant, but she couldn't quite bring herself to disagree. Suddenly, she was terribly tired. No, not tired exactly—she just couldn't wait to get to sleep and see the lady in the water. If there was a link between her dreams and this place, then the best place to figure it out was in her sleep.

✦

Upstairs, Maris tossed her backpack into a chair, took a warm shower, and fell promptly into a fitful and unpleasant sleep.

She had hoped she'd dream of the well, and the lady in the water, and she did. But this dream was unlike any she could remember ever having before—and it was not one she hoped she would ever repeat. It was twisted and frightening, and not at all the lovely meeting that had been teasing from the back of her thoughts ever since she'd arrived in Havenwood Falls.

In the dream, it was dark. Not nighttime exactly, but even darker than that, as if the sun had forgotten how to shine and darkness had eclipsed the world so completely that even a memory of sunlight didn't dare to peep through. And it was cold—terribly, terribly cold. So cold that even the fog of sleep couldn't shield Maris from feeling the icy breath of the air around her. Her bones ached with the sting of it, and paired with the unending blackness, she could have just as easily been standing in the absence of space rather than the middle of a frozen forest. Nothing grew. There was no scent of flowers in the air—there was no scent of anything, really, but the cold itself. It was so cold that the evidence of the lush plant life that had previously been in this place wasn't even white, but gray. Frozen and sullen and dull.

The well was there, as it always was, but it, too, was changed. Like the world around it, the well was dark and cold, but it was these things in a way that had little to do with light or temperature. The water was not frozen, but it was slick and cold. It was a hard thing to explain, but it was as if all the warmth—not just the physical kind but the sort suffused with the love and allure that had always made the well's water thick and comforting in Maris's dreams—had been drained from it, so that she could see without touching that the water had become startlingly thin, its life sucked away both in terms of its substance and its contents, becoming so low that even when Maris leaned over the side of it, her fingertips could not graze the water's surface. Slivers of ice floated menacingly on the water's surface, sharp and pointed like little frozen daggers awaiting something to cut. Something else glittered atop the water, decorating the edges of the stones where the water lapped against them. Maris touched one of the sparkling crystals and brought it to her lips. Salt. It was as if the well was full of tears.

"Where are you?" Maris called out in her dream, the wet words sticking to her lips like ice chips as they tumbled down into the bottomless darkness of the well. Her eyes scanned the shadows for the woman, watching the water for movement—for a sign of her milk-white skin or flaming red hair that might bring color into the black void. "What has happened to you? I'm here. I'm trying to find you. Please come to me."

Maris hadn't realized it at first, but she was crying. Most of the tears froze on her cheeks before they could fall, but one escaped, tumbling down the side of her face and lighting upon the top of the semi-frozen water with an audible clink. Its arrival stirred the first movement since Maris had arrived in her dream.

She stared into the dark as a darker shadow filled the belly of the well. Blacker and denser than the water, it swelled upward, bringing along with it a tangle of a thousand swirling shadowy tentacles, each winding their way around the mass, reaching for the water's surface. As the figure rose, so did a heavy, sickly feeling in the pit of Maris's stomach, and she put her palm over her mouth to keep a scream from finding its way out. She shouldn't be scared, but she was—she was terrified, but couldn't force herself to look away. Something was wrong. Horribly, horribly wrong. Whatever was coming was not the beauty she'd become infatuated with, the woman who had captured her heart in a series of nighttime moments she could only imagine were real. In her heart, Maris knew that this figure coming had something to do with her beloved, but it carried nothing of her light or her spirit. Whatever had become of her, she was now darkness incarnate, and Maris finally found enough energy to stumble backward. As she did, her heel caught on a snarl of hard gray bramble, and she tumbled to the ground, unable to do anything but watch as the darkness rose above the outer rim of the well.

The scream that Maris had kept hushed behind her palm stalled in her throat as she saw what emerged above the well's surface. It had the same face of her love—the same bone structure, the same taunting lips

—but it belonged now to something else entirely. Like the world around, the color had drained from the woman, replacing her beauty with the pallid mark of a corpse. Her skin was deathly white, a gray so deep it was almost blue, and her lips had shriveled into tight, wet black smudges. Eyes that had once been vibrant green had lost their hue so that it was impossible to tell the iris from the pupil as they scanned the area in an unseeing, sweeping gaze. Her body had shriveled beneath her white gown so that her once curvaceous form was reduced to a collection of skeletal knobs and angles, and her hair, her beautiful long curling strawberry hair, was now knotted and tangled, writhing like a mass of black snakes around the place where her sharp, talon-like hands clawed at the base of the well.

The woman that Maris had loved lifted her face upward, as if scenting Maris's presence, and when her unseeing eyes landed on Maris, she could feel them, cold and sharp and hateful, on her skin. Then, before Maris could so much as react, the woman opened her mouth, wide and black, and screamed.

"Come away with me," the figure screamed.

Her—whatever she had become—voice was so sharp and piercing that it shattered the dream. Maris's eyes snapped open in the pale darkness of her bedroom in the turret, which by comparison was not very dark at all and very, very warm. She gasped, panting and shaking, trying to shake off her terror as her eyes adjusted to the room around her. Her hands ran the length of her body as if trying to reassure her that what she had dreamt had been nothing but a nightmare—a stressful reaction, perhaps, to her sudden departure from Denver, and Graham, and all she had left behind—but even as she was on her way to believing this lie, Maris's hands found that the truth of the dream might be much stranger.

A shudder of panic punctuated her breath as Maris's fingertips ran across a patch of ice on her bed sheets, the same salty coldness as the frost she found lingering on the skin of her face. She opened her lips to cry out, but her throat was choked, filled with a tangled clump of wet black hair.

CHAPTER 7

*W*hen Maris awoke several hours later, she could only vaguely remember her nightmare. The most she could recall was a sense of being frightened, and cold, and possibly wet (and not in the enjoyable way), but she didn't have the foggiest recollection of why. She did, however, clearly remember the ice, and the hair, although both seemed to have vanished. Now it was early—the small clock on her bedside table said it was nine in the morning, which was several hours earlier than Maris normally woke—and the sun was shining brightly outside, but there was a weird darkness that clung to Maris's bones despite the beautiful morning waiting on the other side of her bedroom window. She could have rolled over and gone back to sleep, and maybe even caught another hour to two, but she was ready to get up.

Despite the fact that she knew it would be a warm waning spring day, Maris was uncommonly cold when she wriggled her way out from beneath the pile of blankets on her bed. Luckily, she'd tossed a light jacket in her backpack—the kind that could be zipped up into its own little pouch—and so she pulled on her jeans and a fresh T-shirt and added the jacket over the top. Her hair had been wet when she'd gone to bed, so it was a lively tangle of unruly curls, but that was an easy fix, too. She swept the stray curls up into a messy bun, gave her face and teeth a quick scrub, and applied a quick slick of lip gloss as she descended the stairs without bothering to check her phone. It had been much too late yesterday when she'd arrived in Havenwood Falls —a town she'd already decided kept an early bedtime—to do much exploring, but with the day young, she figured she could cover a lot of ground before making her way back to Fallview Tavern and Grille and finding out if she really had a job or if Simon had just been flirting with her.

About halfway down the stairs, Maris decided that her obvious first visit should be to the falls themselves—the ones she'd seen in the banner on the shuttle that had lured her to Havenwood Falls yesterday. Sure, that was literally *right* at the tavern, but whatever. It'd be a nice round trip. Maybe there was a map of the area at the front desk, some kind of basic layout of the town they might give the tourists or something that would show her where all the best places to visit might be. She was especially interested in checking out the scenery, particularly the water. She'd start at the falls and maybe see what else she could find. The chill in her bones got just a little bit cooler when she thought this, as if encouraging her.

Arriving in the lobby area, the first thing Maris saw was a familiar face. Without meaning to, a wide smile spread across her face—the kind that had the tendency to draw people to her like moth to a flame whether she wanted it or not—and the coldness in Maris's bones heated into something much warmer.

Simon.

Sitting with him were Michaela Petran—who smiled and rose as Maris approached, then returned to her station behind the front desk —and another girl who wore librarian's glasses and a diamond stud piercing in her nose, both of these offset by a colorful jumble of tattoos that marched up and down her arms like a circus parade. She looked at Maris anxiously as she approached, but Simon's face wore the same calm expression he'd had last night.

Maris's smile faltered as Simon waved her over, gesturing to a plate of pastries and a steaming coffee carafe set upon the table. The chick sitting with him looked friendly enough, but there was something about her that suggested this wasn't an accidental meeting, and Maris wondered what she was in for. Curiosity flared in her.

Maris would have died a long time ago if she'd been born a cat.

"Morning," Simon said, as Maris reached the table and settled herself into Michaela's vacated chair. As Maris surveyed the food, her stomach growled. Then she remembered she'd skipped dinner, and that the last food she'd had was the truck stop cheese sandwich she wasn't even sure she'd finished. Usually, she couldn't sleep on an empty stomach, but this morning she could barely even remember her head hitting the pillow.

Maris returned the greeting, and then a thought struck her. "I'm not late, am I? I thought I wasn't supposed to be at the Grille until tonight?"

Simon smiled. "Not late. I'm early. Found myself out this way and thought I'd swing by. Glad to see you made it to the inn all right."

Maris shrugged, grabbing what looked like a cinnamon scone from the platter on the table. "This looks great. I didn't know they served breakfast here, but I'm starving."

Simon laughed and ran a hand through his curls in a way that looked automatic as Maris dove into the pastry, groaning audibly as the sweet bread filled her mouth with notes of cinnamon and cardamom. "Well, then, tuck in. All these goodies aren't going to eat themselves. Baked fresh this morning down at the Daily Knead. Great sandwiches and stuff for lunch, too, if you're interested."

Nodding, she reached for the carafe, but the girl with the tattoos had her fingers around its grip first and had already begun to fill Maris's cup, then top off her own and Simon's. Setting it back on the little paper doily on the table, she pushed the little pots of cream and sugar in Maris's direction.

"I guess I'll introduce myself." She winked, smiling brightly as she gave her head a little tip in Simon's general direction. "My name's Adelaide Beaumont, but my friends call me Addie. Welcome to Havenwood Falls."

Maris wiped the crumbs from her fingers and accepted Addie's handshake, only barely glancing at Simon. Simon may have been the mutual friend, but this was very clearly girl time.

"I'm Maris—just Maris. Maris Heilen. Nice to meet you, too." Then, selecting another, smaller piece of what might have been a sectioned Danish, she asked, "So what brings you to the inn first thing in the morning? Are you Simon's girlfriend or friends with Michaela?"

Simon looked as if he was about to say something, but Addie interrupted, a small laugh lifting her words. "No, and yes. Simon says you just arrived last night, on the shuttle from Grand Junction. How are you settling in?"

"Great, thanks. I'd thought I'd just stay the night, but looks like I might hang around a while. Simon even offered to let me bartend at Fallview. Michaela set me up with a sweet room here. Already feels like home."

"That's Havenwood Falls for you," Addie agreed, and Maris wondered if there was another meaning hiding out in her words.

"It's been less than twenty-four hours, and everyone has been so nice. Seriously, I've shown up in a lot of places without a plan, and this has been the nicest greeting I think I've ever had. Most folks don't care at all when a stranger shows up, but it's like you all having some kind of welcoming committee or something. It's a little like I've stumbled into an episode of *The Twilight Zone*—just a really, really nice one." Maris winked when she said it so the comment didn't get misinterpreted as rudeness or arrogance. Still, there was some truth in her words. Michaela and Jakeel had also seemed to know too much about her for someone who'd just walked into town, and they'd gone out of their way to help. Simon had given her a job based on a flirt. And there'd been that strange way that Odette Alverson looked at her and then agreed to hire her, skills unseen. Maris got that it was a small town and good news traveled fast, but this seemed *really* fast.

For a split second, Addie looked taken aback, but then she smiled and tapped her fingertip to her temple. "Got a sense about these things," she joked.

Having polished off her first mug of stout black coffee, Maris laughed as she refilled her cup. She took a closer look at Addie, with her light brown hair tucked under a black beanie, her skin decorated with more tattoos and piercings and pieces of jewelry than Maris could count. She was wearing a black tank top with a pentagram on it, black ripped jeans, and black combat boots, but for all her rough edges, Maris could see herself becoming fast friends with Addie Beaumont.

"What are you, some kind of witch?" she teased.

Addie grinned a particularly mischievous-looking grin and elbowed Simon, who Maris had almost forgotten was there. "Exactly."

✦

By the time the trio had finished the coffee—including a second pot, which Michaela had delivered before joining in the conversation until another guest called away her attention—and eaten their fill of breakfast pastries, Maris was quickly starting to fall in love with this little town and its quirky inhabitants. And so, when Addie pulled out the traveling tattoo kit she "always carried with her" and offered her a free tattoo right there on the spot, Maris had a really hard time thinking of a reason to say no.

She did hesitate, though. Tattoos were permanent, and Maris had never been one to say yes to anything forever, even ink. She'd managed to go her whole life without a single tattoo, and she relayed this to Addie, who waved away her objection as she assembled pieces of her kit and set out some ink on the tabletop. Simon cleared away the dishes to give them more room, and, perhaps, some privacy.

"We can totally do a temporary one," Addie reassured her. "If it fits, after a while, we can always make it permanent, or not. Up to you."

Options. Maris liked options. A temporary tattoo was just the thing: fun to wear for now, and she could decide what to do with it when she felt ready. "Okay," she said, "I'm in."

Addie buzzed the tattoo gun and wriggled her eyebrows encouragingly while Maris bit her lip in excitement. "What's it gonna be, Maris?" Addie asked. "You pick, or it's dealer's choice."

It took Maris less than three seconds to decide, which wasn't so much as a decision, really, as an image that flashed instantly across her thoughts. She unzipped the jacket and pulled her left arm out, offering her upturned wrist to Addie.

"A North Star," she said, touching the fingers of her right hand to the area of skin right above the folds in her skin from her wrist.

With the steadfast attention of a true artist, Addie held Maris's wrist with one hand and rubbed an ointment on her skin at the selected spot. For several moments, she didn't say anything, then, as she began to etch the design on Maris's skin in a shade of ink that was not the traditional black Maris had expected, she said something that made Maris's heart skip a beat.

"You know, there's an old legend in Havenwood Falls about a woman with a tattoo just like this one—a North Star on her inner wrist," she said.

Maris's hand clenched and unclenched of its own accord, and the chill she'd felt that morning breathed coolly over her skin. She slipped her free arm back into her jacket. "Really?"

Addie, her eyes still on the tattoo that was taking shape on Maris's wrist, nodded. "Yes. Well, not a woman exactly. A naiad, actually—a water spirit that granted blessings to those who sought her out in the well where she lived, somewhere deep in the forest. They said if you saw the naiad, she'd give you some of her magic and you would keep it with you, blessed in love for the rest of your years."

Maris's heart was racing, and she hoped Addie wouldn't notice her pulse beating wildly in her wrist.

"What was her name?" she asked, her voice breathy and uneven.

This time, Addie met her eyes, shining from behind her black-rimmed glasses. "Her name was Noelani, but she isn't called that anymore."

Noelani. Now that Maris heard the name, she remembered it. She'd whispered it a million times in her dreams to the woman in the well.

"Why?" Something in Addie's eyes made the breath that was stuck in Maris's throat turn hard, uncomfortable. She gulped, jerking as the needle in Addie's tattoo gun pierced her wrist in a sensitive spot.

"Well," Addie continued, "legend has it that Noelani was once a beautiful creature, full of love and blessings, until one day many years ago—in the seventies, I heard—a woman was drowned in Noelani's well by her fiancé. It is said that as Noelani watched the woman die, all of the love inside her died out. She was, like, made sick by the rage and betrayal of it all, and she became something dark and evil."

The chill in Maris was so strong that her skin had grown pale. Remnants of last night's dream—no, last night's *nightmare*—crept back into her thoughts, and for the first time since she'd opened her eyes that morning, she remembered the monstrous wraith that had crawled out of the well. She remembered the sense of emptiness, too, and the feeling that all life and light had been sucked away.

"Where is Noelani now? Can she ever return to the way she was?"

Addie didn't answer at first. She was busy putting the finishing touches on Maris's tattoo, which looked so similar to the one Maris had seen in her dreams that it might have been copied from a picture rather than sketched from an idea.

"I don't honestly know," she admitted finally, with a shrug. "That's where the legend more or less ended. Naiads can't survive without water, even when they've turned into something else, and that's what she is now—something else. The name we use for Noelani now is rusalka. It means a malicious spirit that lives in the water, because that's what she is, Maris. She's no longer the beautiful thing she once was, but something full of anger and hate."

The story had ceased to be mere legend, and now it sounded as if Addie was warning her about something—someone—very real here in Havenwood Falls. "But she wasn't always that way. Couldn't she go back to the way she was before?"

Addie shrugged again. "Some say a pure enough love could bring her back to herself, but others say that she's lost forever. No one has ever dared to find out."

"What do you mean, 'dared to find out'?"

Addie screwed up her face and shook her head, as if she was clearing her thoughts like an Etch-A-Sketch. "Oh, I don't know. It's just an old story, after all."

Maris wasn't letting it go. "But still, what does the story say would happen if someone tried, you know, tried to bring Noelani back?"

Addie pursed her lips like she didn't want to answer. When she didn't, Maris tapped her fingers against the other woman's knee in a gentle prod. "Oh, all right. Two things could happen. One, if the person who tries to save Noelani is pure of heart, she'll return to how she once was. That's the best case scenario. Worst case is that the rusalka pulls the person down into the well with her—forever."

Maris had gone from chilled to freezing. She attempted to pour a fresh cup of coffee to warm her up, but the carafe was empty. She decided against any further line of questioning in that direction and changed course.

"And what happened to the fiancé?" Maris asked. "The man who drowned the woman he was supposed to marry—what happened to him?"

Since she'd finished the tattoo, Addie had turned to clean her tattoo gun. At this question, she shrugged again. "Well, that's the saddest part, I think . . . and the most fitting. Remember I told you that those who saw Noelani would take some of her magic with them?"

Maris nodded.

"Well, he saw her—or rather, she saw him. No one really knows what happened, but it's said that he left Havenwood Falls with some of Noelani's darkness inside him. He would have spent the rest of his days cursed and eventually the darkness would have swallowed him up as much as it swallowed up Noelani."

As the story of Noelani and her well and her consuming darkness unwound itself in Maris's mind, she began to feel that somehow, her dreams of Noelani were more than just dreams. Somehow, the fate of the woman in the well was tied to her own.

"What was his name?" she asked, her voice barely more than a whisper.

"Who?" Addie asked, refusing to make eye contact.

"The man who drowned his bride," Maris clarified, "who cursed the naiad—what was his name?"

"Oh, I don't think—"

Maris found her voice again, and her words were firm. "What was his name?"

With a deep sigh, Addie put the tattoo gun down in its case and finally met Maris's eyes. She took Maris's hand in hers, examining her work. "Well," she said, sliding her fingers over the fresh tattoo before turning Maris's hand over and letting her fingers continue their journey on the life lines of Maris's palm. "That's the strange thing, isn't it? According to the story, the man's name was Heilen. Peter Heilen."

CHAPTER 8

*U*ntil now, Maris had only fainted once in her life, and that was when she'd first heard her father had died. Even then she wasn't entirely convinced it was the shock of the news of his death that had caused her to faint, mostly because she'd done so hours before she got the official call. The time that she'd fainted matched almost exactly the time the coroner would eventually determine the man had passed. It was several hours later when someone from the police department had phoned to check for next of kin and invite her, hesitantly, to identify the body in the morgue—a request she'd politely declined to do in person and, instead, conducted over the sterile safety of a video call. Maris hadn't been close to her father in years—or, really, ever—but his death had hit her nonetheless, stinging somewhere deep within her core in a place she seldom visited. She'd dropped on the spot, right behind the bar where she'd been slinging drinks and chatting up a full panel of tipsy men who were just drunk enough to tip her well without harassing her. Even though she hadn't spoken to her father in nearly a year, Maris had felt like something within her had been ripped away when Peter Heilen died. That—the loss, not his death—was what Maris long believed had made her faint, as if his sudden vacancy had affected her and was trying to pull a piece of her along with him. Like something inside of her was bound to something inside of him.

Now, reopening her eyes in her bedroom in the turret at Whisper Falls Inn in the surreal little town of Havenwood Falls, Maris again wondered if it had been her father's death that tore away a piece of her when he'd died, or if his departure from the mortal timeline had caused something else entirely to begin a long-awaited unraveling within her, a slow undoing that had been initiated, somehow, by his passing. Her dreams had taken on a different sort of urgency then, and this had all coincided with the time Maris had first started thinking about leaving Graham, and Denver, behind. Since then it had all festered, some deep yearning pulling her away from the life she had known and toward something else. She'd fallen in love with the woman in the dream as if she'd been a real person, crying out to her. Now, Maris wasn't typically the sort of girl that kept her feet on the ground, but even for her, the possibility that she could be a part of something so magical and mysterious was almost completely inconceivable. What was the saying, truth is stranger than fiction? It was simply all too bizarre to be real.

Whether dream or fiction or something else, this was all just a bit much, Maris decided, harrumphing disagreeably as she rolled onto her side. She had always had a suspicion that her dreams were more than what they seemed, but this . . . this was unbelievable—that the woman she'd been dreaming of her was tied to her, by what? A magical curse? Because her father had murdered a woman he had promised to marry, sometime before Maris herself had been born? It was impossible, preposterous. In the stunning brightness of the midday sun, Maris wasn't even sure the events of this morning had happened at all. They felt far away and only vaguely believable, and maybe as if they'd been nothing more than another one of her strange, too-real dreams. It was hard to rationalize a legend lurking within your real life under the best of circumstances, but it was another thing altogether to find yourself right in the middle of living out a full-on twisted fairy tale.

No, that couldn't be true. This wasn't a fairy tale, and Maris's dreams were just dreams—events of her overstimulated imagination, as

Grim Graham had once suggested. Clearly, she'd gone off the deep end —no pun intended. Either that, or her new "friends" in Havenwood Falls were having a hell of a time hazing her. She'd have to reconsider her recent infatuation with this strange little town. Maybe what she needed to do was to get out of this inn, find the shuttle back to Grand Junction, get right back in her car, and keep going west toward . . .

Toward what? She'd been letting the current take her west. Toward water. Toward the woman that may or may not really exist that she'd managed to somehow fall in love with through a series of recurring dreams that felt too real. If they *were* real—and if Havenwood Falls was truly linked to her, the woman called Noelani—then Maris had no choice but to stay and find her. That is, unless she'd gotten food poisoning or something from that gross gas station food and had been sleeping off the sickness through a series of weird hallucinations and crazy thoughts. A whole lot less mystical, that possibility was distinctly more rational. Logic had never been her best friend, but right now she couldn't let her emotions get the best of her, either.

✦

Maris lay in bed silently for a few moments considering this strange turn of fate and arguing with herself. She had almost resolved that the events of the past two days—particularly, the weirdness of this morning—had been just another odd dream before she realized that this wasn't her first time to wake up this morning. She was fully dressed, wearing the same jeans and shirt she'd put on in her "dream." Something itched on her wrist, and Maris pulled at the sleeve of her jacket to reveal the tattoo Addie Beaumont had given her: a North Star, which matched exactly to the woman in her dream. As if these things weren't evidence enough that the morning's events had not been fantasy, Maris discovered, much to her surprise, that she was not alone.

Simon was in her room, although Maris suspected that he was only pretending to be asleep from his position in the sitting chair that was placed, incidentally, at the lip of the turret window. This provided the room a breathtaking view of the town, and beyond it, the thick forest that hugged the falls. The high sun indicated it must have been around noon, and Maris was less surprised about finding a man in her bedroom (that had happened on more than one occasion, though her guest was typically in her bed beside her and not fully clothed on the other side of the room) than she was at the fact that she had failed to lose herself staring at the view outside her window before.

Sitting up in her bed and listening over the sounds of Simon's steady breathing, Maris learned she could indeed hear the whisper of the falls as they fell in the distance, and as she took in the sound of the falls she almost thought she could make out words on the water, like the whisper was not merely the sough of the water, but a voice. The woman—Noelani—Maris knew, was not in the falls but in a well in some forgotten place on the edge of a forest that she had never been. Perhaps she was calling to her, in a very literal way, from the water?

Maris groaned loudly and let her head fall into her fingers. Rubbing her temples, she told herself to get it together. She was starting to question her own sanity. A naiad calling to her inside the sound of water? *Please.*

"You're awake." Simon's voice spoke over the water's.

"I've had the weirdest dreams," Maris spoke from inside her hands. She inhaled a few calming breaths before parting her fingers so her eyes could find Simon's in the space in between. "You were in them. And now you're in my room." Clarity finally arrived, and with it, shock. "Why are you in my room?"

As if such a thing were completely normal, Simon yawned, stretching his legs to their full length out before him. "You fainted," he said simply. "Michaela thought such a sight might be bad for business, so I carried you up. Put you in bed. Figured it'd be better that you didn't wake back up alone and confused, but I must have fallen asleep waiting. Sorry if my being here is weird for you."

Dropping her hands, Maris sighed. "It's not. I mean, it *is.* Everything is." She stared at the temporary tattoo on her wrist, choosing her next words carefully before she spoke them. "Is it true? The story Addie told me—is it really just a legend, or . . ." Her words trailing off, she waved her hands in the air in front of her as if to say,

"Is it all true? Did my father really murder someone? Are there really such things as naiads?" and the most frightening question of all, "What is my part in all of this?"

Simon nodded as he pulled himself upright, then rose from the chair and, with a quick look out the window, relocated himself to the corner of Maris's bed. He raked long fingers through his unruly curls again before patting his hand gently on the bend of Maris's knee. He opened his mouth as if to say something, reconsidered it, and started again.

"Havenwood Falls is a unique place," he began. "There are many legends here—many of which are true, many of which are not, and many of which are only half known and still mostly mystery. I can't say with any certainty exactly what happened at the well, or to the creature that lives within it, or even whether the story as we know it is anything more than fiction. But there is a reason you are here, Maris. Something brought you to Havenwood Falls. The biggest question is what are you going to do now that you're here and you know there's a reason you found this place."

"I don't know," Maris admitted, her eyes moving from the man at the foot of her bed to the glimpse of water in the distance outside her window. She laughed, and the sound was hard. "I want to believe this is all a fantasy. Maybe I got into a car wreck and I'm in some kind of coma or something."

Simon smiled. "Maybe."

Maris's second laughter was softer when it came through her lips. "But part of me knows I'm not dreaming. This is real. Whatever this is, it's real." She felt the truth of it as she spoke it, and another thought occurred—a question for which she desperately needed an answer. "Is she real? The woman—the naiad—Noelani? And . . . is she really a naiad?"

"Yes. She is real, or at least she was. And she was a naiad. I'm afraid I don't know much more."

Maris stared intently at the man on her bed until her eyes found her way to his—blue and iridescent and slightly glassy. "So if naiads are real in this place, then what are you? Your eyes don't look human."

Again, Simon smiled, and as if by way of answer, he blinked. It took Maris a moment to comprehend what she'd seen and then he blinked again and she saw it clearly this time—an inner eyelid sliding over his pupil so that it wet the eye underneath without fully closing, similar to a cat's eye, or a reptile's.

"I'm a dragon shifter." He grinned, and Maris could see it. It was hard to define what *it* was exactly, but there was something distinctly dragon-y about him.

She swallowed hard. Maris had always been the type to believe human beings were not the only creatures to walk the planet, but meeting one was . . . different. "And what am I?"

To her relief, Simon's eyes blinked like a human's this time, and the chill that had seeped into her bones dissipated. "That remains to be seen."

Maris muttered "Okay" under her breath about a dozen times before replying. *Cool.* So not only were supernatural critters real, but she might be one herself. Actually, it kind of made sense. She'd never quite fit in anywhere, no matter how hard she looked. Maybe that was why.

"Can you take me to her well?" she asked.

Simon shook his head and in one, smooth motion, rose to his feet and extended a hand. "No, but I know who can."

"Is she a dragon . . . or a naiad . . . or whatever, too?" The fact that she'd said that sentence was too weird for Maris to think about.

"Oh, no." Simon laughed as he gave Maris's hand a gentle squeeze. "She's something much worse."

CHAPTER 9

Odette Alverson was tall, elegantly beautiful, and completely intimidating. Maris could feel the other woman's pale blue eyes follow her every move as she made her way behind the bar in Fallview Tavern & Grille, listening intently as Simon instructed her on both the town and the operations of the restaurant. There was a sharp, curious look in the proprietress's eyes, and every time Maris caught a glimpse, she wavered in her assessment of whether the look was curious or cruel. Something about Odette Alverson was deeply unsettling and, simultaneously, totally alluring.

Simon had directed Maris to Odette as a source of information, but thus far Maris had been unable to summon the courage to speak to the woman. It was rare that she was overawed by anyone, and even more rare that it would be enough to make her keep her distance when her insides were burning with questions. Still, while Odette had given Maris a friendly wave when she'd arrived and done nothing to dissuade her questions, Maris had clung behind the bar instead, milking as much information as she could from the only person in Havenwood Falls Maris might actually consider a friend. It helped that he was a man, too. Usually, men found opening up to Maris irresistible. In fact, she'd learned more than she wanted to know from the lips of overly chatty men. Unfortunately, no matter how many smiles she gave

Simon or how she accidentally let her arm brush up against his, this dragon man remained frustratingly tight-lipped. They'd been at the bar for hours—indeed the setting sun was already tinting the sky pink—and she didn't feel like she'd learned anything more than she had that morning in the inn.

Maris found it helped to temper her questions—and Simon's perpetually cryptic answers—about Havenwood Falls with brainless chatter about bar operations, a subject Maris suspected she might actually know more than Simon about. She couldn't tell if Simon was being vague on purpose when he deflected her incessant questions about the town, the well, or her father, or if he simply didn't have any good answers to give. It was either a very big secret, or information was shared strictly on a need-to-know basis, and Maris was on the wrong side of that need.

"Okay," Maris said finally, waving the bar towel in her hand over her head in a sign of surrender. "Is there *anything* else you can tell me?"

"No," Simon insisted, for what must have been the millionth time that evening, though he'd never once shown he was anything other than patient with her questioning. He tossed his head back over his shoulder, nodding toward Odette, who was busy not listening as she sorted menus at the hostess station. "But *she* can."

Maris flung the towel down on the countertop with an exasperated sigh. "*Fine*," she relented. Then, summoning her courage, she made her way to the other side of the tavern.

Odette turned as Maris arrived, brandishing what looked to be a genuine smile under critical eyes. "Maris," she greeted her coolly.

"Hi . . ." Maris stammered, then collected herself. "Look, I know this probably sounds crazy or whatever—"

"Your tattoo," Odette cut in, holding her hand out to accept Maris's arm. "May I see it?"

Maris didn't know what else to do but comply, and so she did, holding back a shiver as Odette's fingers—which were as cool as her voice—traced around the star Addie had added to Maris's wrist.

"I had thought," she whispered, speaking as if to herself, "but I wasn't sure to believe. But it is true. You are the child of Peter Heilen, and, it would appear, bound to his fate as well."

Maris gulped, retrieving her arm from the woman's grasp. Her touch gave Maris the shivers, and she'd been having a tough time feeling warm already. "So it's true then? The legend of the naiad in the well? That my father . . . murdered someone?"

"It would appear so." There was no emotion or judgment in Odette's voice when she said this. It was simply a statement of fact.

"Are you"—Maris cleared her throat to push through the insanity she was about to say—"are you a naiad, too?"

"No," Odette answered in a voice just as cool and emotionless as before. "I have a very different relationship with the water."

The way she said it told Maris in no uncertain terms that further inquiry on that particular topic was off limits. There were a few beats of silence, and then Odette asked a question of her own. "Tell me, have you ever been in love before, Maris?"

Maris blinked at the strange question, which was not at all in line with where she thought this conversation was going. "In love?"

"Yes, in love. Have you ever truly loved someone? Anyone—a family member, a friend, anyone?"

Maris didn't have to think of an answer. She knew it already. "No," she said, shaking her head with a derisive laugh. "Lust, yes. I've had a lot of that. I've cared about people, but I can't say I've ever really loved anyone. I just have never been able to bring myself to be able to. Except . . ."

Her voice trailed off, and Odette's eyes widened, anticipating an answer. "Except?"

Clearing the way for another crazy thought to take form in her throat, Maris sighed. "Except her. Noelani. I love her. I don't know how, or why, and I'm not even sure I know what love feels like, but . . . I love her. It's ridiculous, really. I'm not even attracted to women, or at least I never have been—not in that way. But I see her and I think of her and I get this movement in my chest that sort of hurts but feels amazing at the same time, and all I want to do is *be* with her. It's like a sickness that I don't want to get better from. It's not infatuation. It's not lust. I know what those feel like. This is . . . different. I don't even know if she's real, but I love her."

"Oh, Noelani is very real," confirmed Odette, who breezed over the particulars as she continued to home in on her point. "But tell me, what do you know of her?"

Maris shrugged. "Only what Addie told me, really, and I can barely believe that. It's all so strange—no offense." Unfortunately, Maris had no idea who or what she was talking to anymore when she chatted up the residents in Havenwood Falls.

If any offense to what Maris had said was taken, Odette didn't let it show. "No. I don't mean what you've *heard* of her, or the stories you've been told or what you might have read about naiads and rusalki in a storybook, but what you know of *her*."

At first, Maris wasn't sure she understood what the other woman meant, and then it dawned on her. "I dream about her," Maris said, feeling warmth creep up her cheeks and color them red. "A lot, actually. I have for as long as I can remember, but lately the dreams have been . . . different."

Nodding, Odette confirmed this was an appropriate answer. "And how is she in these dreams?"

"Beautiful. Kind," Maris said automatically, the blush crawling its way down her neck in a wandering sort of trail that was not missed by Odette's gaze. "In my dreams, she loves me back."

"Then there is hope."

"Hope?"

"Yes," Odette breathed, drawing her hand to her chest. For a moment, she seemed to let her thoughts percolate on a conversation that mostly just confused Maris, her fingers drumming against her breastplate, then her hand dropped to her pocket, and she pulled out a crinkled piece of paper. "Like Simon, I don't have all the answers"— Maris bit her lip, feeling slightly guilty for how much she'd pestered the guy and how shamelessly she'd tried to flirt her way to answers— "but I can add what I know about Noelani's curse. She was, as Addie said, once very beautiful, and very loving. But when Heilen—when your father—drowned his bride-to-be in her well, the rage and suffering of it cursed them both. For Noelani, it blackened her heart and made her vengeful and cruel. For your father, well, he saw this when he looked into her eyes. Whatever capacity he had to love and be loved was lost until his own emptiness overtook him. And, it would appear, some of this curse spread to you as well."

"Me?" Maris blinked back her surprise. "But I wasn't even born yet."

"Magic has a way of being passed. It's in your blood," Odette confirmed, unfolding the slip of paper. "You are called to the water, yet removed from it. You are flanked by people who love you, but unable to return their affections. You suck people into your light and snuff them out, and eventually, should you continue down that path, you will find yourself as dry and dead as your father—the life quite literally sucked from your bones—unless you can undo what your father has done and unravel the harm he inflicted upon Noelani."

The softness in Odette's voice hardened over, like liquid turned to ice, as she said this, and Maris took a step backward, her own hand rising as if to shield her from the sting of Odette's words. It was true, unfathomably true, and Maris knew that—she could see the truth of it in her history of wanderings, of broken hearts left behind. Of Graham.

And it hurt.

Odette held the paper out to Maris, and she took it, careful to avoid the other woman's fingers. On it was a grainy black-and-white image of two people. The first, with his pale hair the same shade as hers and an eerie resemblance throughout the nose and mouth, was her father when he had been a young man. The other was a woman. It was not Noelani, but someone else—an exotic beauty with dark, wavy hair and the lengthened eyebrows and almond-shaped eyes of someone who carried the other side of the Atlantic in their genes, although in the blurry image it was hard to tell if she might have been of African descent or perhaps of Middle Eastern heritage. Regardless, she was distinctly beautiful, with a softness in her eyes and smile that signaled she was as lovely of spirit as she had been of face. Underneath their pictures was a more recent addition: a sketch of Havenwood Falls, with a makeshift map that led to Noelani's well. Maris saw that it was connected to, yet totally removed from, any other source of water in the town—a thing set apart and distinct.

Maris ran her fingers over his father's image, feeling him now as much a stranger to her as the woman pictured with him. "My father never mentioned this place. Never mentioned anything about this woman, or any of it. He always seemed haunted by something, but never gave the impression that he even knew what it was."

"He couldn't have," Odette returned. "Our town is protected by magic, and there are memory wards that erase the town from memories, both for the humans that come and visit and the other things that, well, aren't so human, when they leave. It is a necessary precaution, you understand. But sometimes the truth has a way of making itself known. The same magic that makes people forget has a way of making some return, or calling some anew."

A thought struck in Maris' head. "Things that aren't so human? You mean there are more than naiads here? I've heard"—she fought not to glance in Simon's direction—"but I thought . . ."

Odette gave a brief, tight smile, the sort that looked like it had happened by accident. "Yes. Havenwood Falls acts as a sort of haven for supernatural beings—like me and like Simon. Like Addie and even Michaela. Like you."

"Me? I'm not . . ." Maris scoffed. "I'm not *supernatural*."

"Oh, but indeed you are. At least half." Odette's fingers wrapped around Maris's arm and gently turned the tattoo on her wrist upward. "All supes are marked, even if only temporarily. Those that are approved to stay have their marks made permanent."

Maris had that strange feeling of otherworldly vertigo she'd had when she'd reawakened from her fainting spell, and had to laugh. "So Addie really is a witch."

Odette did not confirm nor deny this. Instead she said, "There are many different creatures in Havenwood Falls, and they all have their secrets and enjoy their privacy. It would appear that the legend was true in that your father took some of Noelani's magic when he left and it has passed to you. Your just being here is testament to that. What happens from here on out will determine if you are part naiad or part rusalka, and what sort of consequence your arrival might have on the legend of Noelani, because that much is inevitable." She gave Maris's tattoo a meaningful tap and then released her arm, adding, "We will see if you are here to heal Noelani's broken heart, or if she will simply pull you down into the darkness with her. It is you, Maris Heilen, who will determine your fate."

Her eyes returning to the paper, Maris gazed again at the woman in the picture. She knew that many women had passed through her father's life—women whom he'd been unable to love every bit as much as Maris herself had been unable to love any of the men who had passed through hers. The fact that she'd been born at all was really nothing more than a nod to nature finding its way, and she'd never know why her father had stuck around, particularly after her mother's death. Thinking on it a bit too hard, she decided to abandon the thought. There was no train of thought that would take it to a happy ending. "What was her name?" she asked. "The woman he killed, what was her name?"

"Stella. Stella Malley."

"Did you know her? Did you know my father?"

"I knew them both, for a time. They were visitors, passing through."

"Was she a . . . a supernatural, too?" Maris asked.

Odette's lovely faced produced a patient smile. "No, she was not. Just an ill-fated star, it would seem. Her destiny was written in her name." Odette paused as her thoughts returned to the past and her voice took on a bemused tone as the woman's name slid from her lips. "Stella. A lovely, bright thing, burned out by someone else's darkness when she might have enjoyed the mist of heaven." Odette's gaze quickened and returned to Maris. "Have you ever given any thought to what your name means?" she asked, as another patron walked through the wide double doors of the tavern and began making their way to the hostess stand, marking the end of the conversation. "If not, you should."

Taking one last glance at the portrait of the doomed Stella Malley and completely at a loss as to how she should feel, Maris refolded the piece of paper and slid it into the back pocket of her jeans. She turned to make her way back to the bar, her thoughts weighed down by riddles and legends.

"Oh, and Maris," Odette called. She turned back to the woman, not sure if she wanted to hear more or not. "Be careful. Don't venture to the well on your own, at least not at first. The forest is a lot more complicated to traverse than you might expect."

✦

Desperate to get her thoughts back to somewhat normal, Maris slung drinks at the bar while Simon cooked during the dinner rush, but the map in her back pocket felt like an anchor in her jeans. It pulled her thoughts with it as she sunk deeper and deeper into her reverie, her mind a tangled web of betrayal, love, and magic.

CHAPTER 10

The arms of long, dark shadows wrapped themselves around Maris as she entered the forest. Jakeel had only taken her so far, to the farthest recesses of the edge of the wood, before insisting that he'd go no farther, and she was utterly alone now. She checked her phone and wasn't the slightest bit surprised to see that it had no signal. It had battery life though, and that meant she had a flashlight.

For now, that was enough.

The tattoo on her wrist burned as Maris made her way deeper into the woods, alternating between rubbing the mark with her free hand and using it as a makeshift divining rod that she hoped might lead her toward water. It was cold in the forest, and growing colder as Maris ventured deeper, trying to match the marks on the hand-drawn map to her surroundings under the unsteady light of her handheld, makeshift flashlight. There was no trail or other sort of marker to guide her, and so she simply kept walking as if compelled to do so and hoped she was heading in the right direction. The forest was barricaded by mountains, so if she bumped into rock, she'd gone too far. A warmer jacket would have been nice to shield her from the cold, but she only had the light jacket she'd brought with her and a knit cap she'd found in the backseat of Jakeel's car. Luckily, Maris had her resolve to keep her warm, and that alone had gotten her through tough spots before.

Around her, the woods were cold but not as quiet as she'd expected it to be. Nor were they filled with the usual sounds you'd expect in a forest. There was no patter of animal footsteps nor cry of birds; no scuttling of insects. Even the leaves on the branches of the trees stayed still, their branches muted and unswayed by psithurism. But the forest wasn't silent, either. There was something—a high-pitched sort of gurgle, as if someone had opened their mouth to scream and then stopped, the sound only barely breaking through the silence—a ringing tinnitus that formed an unsettling soundtrack to Maris's journey and filled the space between her footfalls. It was dark, too, darker even than a forest should be at night; the tree canopy was so thickly webbed that not even moonlight nor the twinkling of stars could break through its barriers. The trees themselves cast layer upon layer of shadows, so that things that might have been green or brown or other colors in the daytime were recast in various shades of black— ink, oil, raven, pitch. The only signs of life Maris found in the forest were the eyes she felt focused on her back as she moved, their gazes so intent that she felt them stabbing holes into her body in the darkness.

Cold and shaken, her resolve giving way until she was left clinging to the verge of hysteria, Maris trekked deeper and deeper into the woods until, after a while, the possibility of turning back was every bit as daunting as moving forward. She began to feel the consequence of her impulse coming back to bite her. No matter how desperate she was to find the well or how many questions she had—how much her desire outweighed her fear—it would have been better to wait until morning, when at least she'd have daylight as an ally. Pushing thoughts of the legacy her father had left for her and of what had become of Noelani out of her mind, Maris considered that it had been her impulsive behavior that had gotten her into these sorts of messes in the past. Blaming herself provided the only protection she could muster from the fear that was seeping around the edges of her thoughts as she stomped deeper and deeper into the woods at the very edge of Havenwood Falls, into a place even Jakeel had had to think about before delivering her. It was impulse that had led Maris to Colorado. To Graham. To leaving Graham. To Grand Junction. To here.

But it might also be impulse that saved her, a tiny voice added. Like Odette had said, even forgetting magic had a way of calling you home. Even a curse could be broken. Even darkness could still be lit if someone brought enough brightness.

And so she walked on, mumbling and shivering.

Until she heard footsteps behind her.

The distinct sound of crunching leaves shattered the heavy silence of the forest inches behind Maris's back. Following it came a rumble that might have been mistaken for thunder had it not been closer to the ground and marred by an undercurrent of ragged breathing. Maris froze as the inevitable source of the noise registered in her thoughts, and she heard the growl, her thoughts immediately racing through every beast—real and imagined, because there were apparently no limitations on what might lurk in the shadows of a place like Havenwood Falls—of which she'd ever known: wolves, both the regular kind and the were kind; bigfoots; trolls; the Penghou; hellhounds. Spiders that might weave her into their webs or nefarious tree sprites that feasted on women. Dozens more monsters for which she didn't even have a name, but all of which bore claws and fangs and would very much enjoy the taste of her flesh.

A second growl followed the first, and Maris's fear bled instantly into panic. She ran, the flashlight on her phone shining unfocused light on things she only half saw but which were sure to visit her in her nightmares for years to come. She tore through the bramble, stray branches slicing at her skin as she flung herself through them, tearing through the flimsy fabric of her jacket so that small beads of blood mixed with her sweat. She fell once, but scrambled back to her feet and kept moving as whatever it was that chased her closed the distance between them, its ragged breath and rumbling growl nearly indistinguishable from her own as she tracked the progress of its movement behind her. Maris ran so furiously and for so long that she didn't notice the forest turning to frost around her, or that the darkness had become so dark it had taken on a blue sheen from the cold, or even that she'd completely stopped trying to follow the map at all.

Just when she thought she could not go on—that whatever was

pursuing her would surely win—Maris shoved her way through a final barrier of branches and lost her footing as her shoes slipped on the slick ground of frozen meadow, the space bright and cold and silver under the steady glow of the moon. As she broke free of the forest, the creature behind her screamed, and the sound twisted Maris's head backward as if of its own accord, and she was forced to face her pursuer—a sight she would have much preferred to never see.

Maris's scream matched the beast's as the two sounds joined together in the otherwise silent wood. The thing that had followed her was not a wolf or any other monster she could have imagined— not a bigfoot or a troll or even a spider. It was not a monster at all— or, at least, it did not appear as one. Standing not ten feet from her, tucked within the shadows and spindly branches of the black forest, was a woman. Her jeans were caked in mud and her jacket torn; the knit cap on her head askew and the pale hair beneath it littered with leaves and pieces of bramble that had knit it together to form a bird's nest of tangles. At first, the woman appeared familiar, but completely normal—flesh and blood and as mortally human as Maris herself. But when the woman's face moved from the shadow and Maris could see it clearly, she screamed again, and she was grateful to be on the ground already as her knees gave way beneath her. The face Maris saw staring back at her was her own, only it was twisted and misshapen, its eyes blank black holes and its toothless mouth agape, as if it were nothing more than a crude, unfinished mannequin of herself.

For the second time in as many days, Maris fainted again, her head falling into cold and total darkness as it hit the frozen earth beneath her.

✦

When Maris opened her eyes, the creature in the woods was gone, its figure swallowed up by shadows in the blank space where it had previously stood. The air around her had grown still, and it was now so cold that Maris could see her breath form little tufts of vapor in front of her as she breathed herself back to a state of calm—or something as close to calm as she was currently able to achieve.

Her eyes still locked on the space where that *thing* had been, Maris pulled herself to her feet and patted herself down. Desperate to reclaim her senses, she ran her hands over her head, her face, her chest, her stomach, and her hips, her pulse slowing as she let herself sink back into the familiarity of her body. Odette had warned her that the woods were unfriendly, but nothing could have prepared her for that. Whatever had chased her had been her, but not her, like it was a manifestation of the darkest side of her, or something like that. She didn't want to think about it just now—or possibly ever.

She stared into the darkness once more, but seeing nothing except darkness there, Maris tore her eyes from the forest and, turning, swept her gaze across the meadow she now found herself in. The feeling here was no less terrifying than the woods. If anything, it was more unsettling, though it was hard to explain how. Woods, after all, particularly at night and particularly when traveled alone, are meant to be scary. Meadows are not, but this one was.

The meadow was small, but wide, and had obviously once been lush and beautiful, like a secret garden protected by a ring of forest. Now it was a frozen wasteland, covered in a layer of unnatural permafrost. Everything here was iced in place, but not even as beautiful as that. It was darker, duller, as if it were not frost at all but cobwebs and dust—a sprinkling of gray over perfectly formed wildflowers and thistle that still held their bloom and promise of color underneath a film of decay. There was utter silence here; not even that eerie gurgle pervaded the air. Even the frozen grass that crunched to shards beneath Maris's feet did so soundlessly as she pulled herself up and moved deeper into the meadow, following a beam of moonlight that directed her to the place she'd been seeking. The cold eclipsed any other scent, except the smell of cold itself, and one other thing—salt.

She stuffed the tattered remains of the map into her pocket and—with a steadying breath—retrieved her phone from the forest floor and focused its beam in front of her.

In the center of the meadow stood the well Maris had dreamed about, only like everything else in this place, it was dark and dismal, sheeted in a thick layer of ice that didn't dare so much as sparkle in the moonlight. This version of the well had a slightly familiar feel to it, too, and Maris did her best to swallow the fear that was rising in the back of her throat. She'd seen this before, but the memory was vague and mercurial, and she couldn't quite catch it long enough to decode it. But even if its appearance was not that of some haunted landmark, it was also the same well she'd seen in her dreams for decades—the one in which she'd laughed and loved and kissed the woman she'd been waiting for her entire life. Maris had always assumed that when—*if*—she ever found this place, she'd run to the well and thrust her hands in the water, calling her beloved's name, a name so delicious she could taste the sweetness of it when it crossed her lips. But now she approached the well carefully, guardedly, and wasn't sure if she should be approaching at all.

"Noelani?" Maris called, or at least she tried. The name stuck in the back of her throat and only a small squeak made its way out of her mouth. Maris cleared her throat and took a deep breath, squinting in the darkness. "Noelani?" This time the word was clear, and the sound of it echoed and reverberated, like a noise caught in a wind chime.

Something stirred in the well. Maris could hear the sound of movement, but it was trapped—the sharp sound of something sliding across the ice from underneath a frozen barrier.

"Noelani?" Maris called again, this time sounding brave and natural and almost insistent. She was only a few feet away from the well now, so she could hear as the frozen surface of the water was broken. She could see, clearly, as ten long white fingers with mottled black tips curled around the edges of the stones that lined the well's outer ring. She could see as the top of a head rose above the water and well stones, and she could see the figure that appeared bore a face the pallid gray of a corpse, which was in turn hidden beneath a thick mass of gnarled black hair that snaked around the body that rose beneath it and poured over the sides of the well like hungry seaweed. She could see the white gown that in her dreams had appeared lovely and enticing on the woman's body, but now lay like a burial shroud over a pile of old bones.

She could see Noelani, but she could also plainly see that this creature that rose from the well was entirely changed from the woman she had known in her dreams.

But, as frightening as the wraith she saw rising from the water was, Maris also saw the star tattoo on the inside of its wrist, so she stood rooted to her spot like she, too, had been frozen to the ground as she watched the thing that had once been Noelani lurch and pull itself out over the edges of the well, moving slowly but deliberately as if every contorted thrust of its wrecked body was painful. Dragging her long, water-logged hair behind her, Noelani—though it was hard to call her that—began to emit a low sound as she moved. It was a sound lost somewhere between a scream and a song—not a moan but a word. A single, strained transmission that started softly and began to grow, until, by the time Noelani had pushed herself beyond the boundaries of her well and was making her painful slog across the ground, it was a piercing screech.

"Heilen," the rusalka was screaming. "*Heilen!*"

"Noelani," Maris attempted. "Noelani, it's me. I've come to save you. I've come to—"

Maris's words were cut short when the writhing thing on the ground finally snaked its long, skeletal, black-tipped fingers around her ankle. Through the heavy fabric of her jeans, she could feel their cold, clammy touch, hard and greedy on her leg. There was a pause, as if for a moment perhaps the touch had elicited another type of connection, and then Noelani's hand locked into place on Maris's ankle, the grip tight and unrelenting, and in one smooth motion jerked her so hard she toppled onto the ground as the wraith began to inch her body—wet and clammy and oddly brittle—on top of hers.

"Heilen," Noelani screamed, her voice a strangled, urgent, guttural sort of call—a death howl heard only underwater.

Maris struggled, trying to throw the other woman off, but she was so strong, so forceful, so unremitting as her hands pinched and pulled. When her face loomed only inches above Maris's, she saw a face more horrible than even that of the creature in the woods, for there was nothing but cruelty and malice in the blackened features of the thing that had once been the naiad.

"Noelani, it's me," Maris attempted, but her breath was forced out of her lungs as Noelani snarled above her. Long tendrils wrapped around Maris's body, twisting around her throat and choking off the ability for Maris to do anything other than splutter as the rusalka moved away, her hair acting like a net that drug Maris along with it, toward the well. Panic rushing over her, Maris kicked and thrashed, screaming soundlessly for Noelani to hear her—to *see* her—but it was of no use.

Maris scrambled when the tips of her shoes bumped against the stones of the well, and she thought she heard the sound of the water as Noelani began to descend back into her dark depths, pulling Maris down along with her. She thrashed harder, terror rising within her as a torrent of tangled thoughts spun inside her head and her heart beat itself furiously against the confines of her chest. She was terrified, angry, and desperate . . . and yet there was a strange urge to allow herself be pulled into the well, to not let go of the thing that was dragging her toward a certain, unending darkness. It was a crazy thought, but insistent, and the confusion of it stalled inside Maris's mind, freezing her body along with it. She felt resigned, suddenly, as the first touch of water breathed coldly across her skin, and then, just as she thought that she would drown after all—sucked beneath the water like her mother had been and her father had tried to warn her of —there was a flash of light, blinding in the darkness. This was joined by the sound of wings and the feel of something sharp as it sliced through the bonds that held her, and then Maris was lifted as if by the jaws of life out of Noelani's clutches and airborne, held in the talons of what was undeniably a large blue dragon.

CHAPTER 11

*M*aris didn't say anything when Simon—because that was the only dragon shifter she'd met thus far—delivered her back to the parking lot at the edge of the forest. She didn't say anything while she used the Luber app on her phone and then waited for Jakeel to collect her in his orange hearse and ferry her back to Whisper Falls Inn. And she didn't say anything when Jakeel himself had to help her out of the backseat and into the building, where Michaela and Addie received her with warm blankets and even warmer drinks—the kind that heated you from the inside out.

She didn't utter a single word until she was completely thawed, completely calm, and then—an hour later, when Simon finally returned in fresh clothes and human form—it all came rushing out.

"What the actual fuck," she started. "She didn't even hear me. She didn't see me. She didn't *know* me. I thought I would be able to . . . I don't know, to *fix* her. To make her remember who she was—who she *is*. But she didn't care. She was going to take me into the water with her, to what—drown me? And that *thing* in the woods. What the hell was that? I don't. I can't. I—"

"Maris, take a breath," Simon cautioned, leaning forward to tighten the blanket around Maris's shivering body. Gently, he coaxed the coffee mug in her hand back to her lips. She took a sip, and immediately felt a rush of relaxation flood her.

"Odette did try to warn you," Addie, who was dressed as if she might have been attending a heavy metal rock concert rather than doing disaster intervention at midnight, reminded her. "Any of us would have gone with you had you asked. We are here to help."

"You're here to supervise, in case I'm capable of the same kind of evil my father was," Maris snapped, and felt instantly guilty. "I'm sorry. I didn't mean that. I mean, maybe I did, but I didn't mean it to come out so rudely. You all have been so kind to me." She looked at Simon and gave him a half-hearted smile. He smiled back.

"The 'thing' in the woods was a changeling," Addie continued, unperturbed. "When the light left Noelani's forest, such dark little beasties were able to creep in and make it their own. They are a type of fae—devious, quarrelsome things that prey on those they perceive as weak. They will try to trap you, so they can steal your place in the human world."

Maris gawked at her. "How are you supposed to beat something like that?"

"Changelings aren't beaten," Michaela interjected. "They have a place in this world as much as we do. But you can guard against them."

Addie nodded in agreement. "Faeries can't stand iron, so carry that with you. Changelings, in particular, avoid fire, so having that on hand will ward them off as well."

"Great. So I'll carry a hardware store in my pocket. Anyone know where I can find a blowtorch?"

Simon raised his hand and winked mischievously.

Maris nearly dropped her mug. "You can literally breathe fire?" she asked, but Simon only shrugged. Maris took another sip from her mug and this time felt almost entirely relaxed—as if she hadn't just been chased down by a soul-snatching changeling and then drowned by the woman she loved. Raising the mug to her lips for a third time, she suddenly stopped and considered her company. "I'm sorry, but I can't drink this," she said.

Addie laughed. "It's just tea with a little bit of brandy, I promise. No funny business. Besides," she winked, "it's not my style to trade in potions."

Maris looked at Michaela and decided it would be rude to ask what type of supernatural she was. If she'd wanted Maris to know, she'd have volunteered the information. "Okay. So, tonight was a disaster. How do I get through to Noelani—is it even possible?"

The other three traded glances, and Maris's heart sank. If a witch, a dragon, and a . . . whatever didn't know how to save a naiad from her own darkness, how in the hell was a cursed maybe half-supernatural chick supposed to do any better?

"We don't know," Addie finally admitted. "That is your magic, not ours."

Maris scoffed into her just herbal tea with brandy. "I don't have any magic. A curse, maybe. But that's about it."

Addie rolled her eyes. "Have you ever thought about why you chose the tattoo that you did?"

Maris hadn't. Not really. She wasn't even sure she'd chosen it. She just got it because it was the same as the mark Noelani had on her own wrist, and she said as much.

"But that's not true—at least, not totally," Addie countered. "See, I did some looking in the town archives. All supernaturals have a tattoo —Odette told you that—but Noelani's wasn't a star on her wrist. At least, it wasn't always. Before the event that . . . changed her," Addie said delicately, "her tattoo was something else—a clam with a pearl on its tongue. The star appeared later. After."

"What does that mean?" Maris asked.

"It means," Simon cut in, "that the symbol you chose is important. It's the missing clue to how to break the curse."

Maris shook her head. She sipped more tea and wished it were a potion. She'd take just about any clarity she could get right about now. "Odette said something similar earlier tonight. Something cryptic about my name, or about the power in a name anyway. But I have no idea what she meant. She said Stella Malley was an 'ill-fated star' and that she could have enjoyed the 'mist of Heaven' had it not been for my father, and she said that I should know what my name meant. Does that mean anything to you?" She directed the question to the group.

"Yes," Addie said wisely, and then winked behind her librarian's glasses before pulling her cell phone out of her back pocket. "It means we should consult the almighty Google on name meanings and see if we can connect the dots."

Typing quickly into her phone, Addie launched a series of short investigative bursts, clicking and scrolling and responding to each with facial expressions that ranged from boredom to enlightenment and back again while Maris let her thoughts wander to the last dream she'd had of Noelani—days ago and worlds away in Graham's apartment in Denver—and ignoring the strange nightmare that had come to her on her first night in Havenwood Falls. She remembered the feel of Noelani's lips pressed against hers, the sensation of the water in her well as her body slid inside of it alongside the wet kiss of Noelani's form against hers. Her heart quickened at the need to slip beneath the water and descend into Noelani's world, the place of hers that was hidden away from the rest of the world where the two could be together, alone.

"Got it!" Addie announced, interrupting Maris's daydream.

"What?" the trio asked in unison.

"Odette was right, although it might have saved us all a lot of time —and sleep—if she'd been a wee bit less cryptic about the whole thing. Okay. So, the name Stella does, pretty literally, mean 'ill-fated star.' That got me looking. Maris, your name means 'to heal; of the sea.' Joined, Stella Maris is 'star of the sea'—a phrase symbolized throughout the ages, from ancient interpretations to modern-day religions, with the North Star. It's the one that would act as a guide for those that found themselves upon nighttime waters—a beacon of hope. Noelani has the symbol on her—it's the guiding light calling you to her—and it found you in your dreams. You are the North Star, Maris—the star that can save her, just like the legend says. We just have to figure out how."

"No," Maris said, her lips curving into a smile as she shrugged out of the blanket. "We don't have to figure out how. I just realized I've known how all along." She looked at Simon. "Will you go with me to the meadow in the morning—be my blowtorch, just in case?"

He nodded. "Absolutely."

"Then daybreak," Maris decided, rubbing her wrist as she stared out the window and judged the number of hours until dawn. Five maybe, give or take. "I don't know how, but at daybreak we go and break the curse my father left on Noelani and her well, and see if there's anything to this *pure of heart* thing after all."

CHAPTER 12

*M*aris didn't sleep that night. Instead, she lay in bed, staring at the ceiling and considering if the next day might bring her death or her salvation, and how she might survive a second trip inside a haunted forest filled with changelings and other creatures of the dark that, until yesterday, she would never have even considered to be real. She never did decide—nor did she let herself get lost in the thought that she might fail and find herself resigned to a similar fate as Stella Malley: breathless at the bottom of Noelani's well.

Nevertheless, she had been called by the water, and to the water she would go. So, true to her word, when the first light of dawn crept over the horizon, Maris quit her idle thoughts, flung herself out of bed, and dressed as quickly and warmly as she could manage with her meager supplies. If she survived today, she'd find a way to fetch her car from Grand Junction. If she didn't, well, then it wouldn't really matter, would it?

Addie had loaned Maris a warmer jacket. Michaela had provided her with a pair of soft wool gloves that someone left in the inn's lost and found and a pair of women's hiking boots whose tread had worn dangerously slick, and Maris added these to her jeans and knit cap and called it good. She washed her face, swept her hair back into a low ponytail that wouldn't make the cap crawl up her scalp, and, summoning Simon—who had enjoyed another snooze in the armchair in her bedroom—boldly set off in the direction she'd traveled last night. She didn't need the map this time, which was lucky because it had ripped and smudged when Maris had run in the woods, ending the prior evening in poor shape. Now it was mostly useless, unable to serve as anything more than a painful reminder of the legacy passed down to her by her father. She left the piece of paper on the bedside table and hoped she could undo the damage her father had done. If she couldn't, then someone deserved to pay the price for his sins, and she supposed it would have to be her. It's not like her dreams would let her escape that fate anyway.

✦

The morning was bright, lit by a blazing sun that washed the scenic landscape of Havenwood Falls in a faintly golden glow, as if the town had been dipped in oil and set ablaze, the tips of the treetops pinnacles of reflecting light against a backdrop of white-hot mountain snow. Maris and Simon did not speak as they rode in his pick-up truck to the patch of forest on the outermost edge of town, but it was a comfortable silence—Simon at the wheel, his curly hair twisting out from underneath the brim of his cable-knit cap and fleece-lined denim jacket, and Maris beside him, daydreaming of the woman she hoped to rescue from the other side of darkness.

Jakeel had delivered Maris to a trailhead that joined a large expanse of property to the untamed forest. As Simon killed his truck's engine in that same space this morning, Maris realized she'd never thanked him for saving her the night before, nor asked why he'd been in the forest to begin with.

Staring at the dense patch of woods before them, Maris zipped up her jacket and turned to Simon. "I never thanked you for last night," she began. "How did you know where to find me?"

"It was my pleasure, and"—he tapped the side of his nose with his index finger—"dragon senses." When Maris gawked at him, Simon laughed so hard he had to tap his palm against the steering wheel for emphasis. "It was an easy guess. When you disappeared from Fallview, Odette and I knew there was only one place you could have gone. She sent me after you. You couldn't have been ready to face that—not the forest or Noelani. Not on your own. Not the first time."

Maris had to laugh. "Honestly, I'm not sure I'm ready to face it all again. But I have to. I have to save her." The thought occurred that she'd never really asked Simon if he wanted to join her—she'd just heard fire, thought dragon, and volunteered him along. "You don't have to come with me. I'm sorry, I just kind of forced you along, as if my problems were any of your concern."

Simon winked and swung the driver's side door open, bending down to speak to Maris through the parted space. "It's always handy to have a dragon on your side. Besides, I've got my own beef with this forest. Being here is helping me, too. And if we succeed, having Noelani back will help a lot of people."

Maris wanted to ask what kind of creatures in this forest would have been enough to give Simon pause but decided she didn't really want to know. She opened her door and slid out onto the ground, then moved around the truck to settle in beside Simon in front of the vehicle. Hesitating, Maris rubbed her hand over her tattoo anxiously. "You know," she confided to Simon without looking, "I have absolutely no idea what I'm doing. I'm about to go marching into a haunted forest and try to break a curse I barely know anything about. My ex would have had a lot to say about this, and none of it would have been good. He always said I was too impulsive, and reckless, and that it would probably get me killed one day."

Simon settled his hand on her shoulder and turned her to face him. "Sounds like now's the time to prove him wrong."

Maris looked into Simon's kaleidoscopic dragon eyes and wondered if it was possible to fall in love for the first time with two different people, neither of which were entirely human, or if this was simply what it was like to truly find a place where you belonged. "I think you and I are going to get along just fine."

Letting his hand slide down her arm, he gave her hand a reassuring squeeze. "Come on, Maris Heilen, let's go see if we can't get some darkness out of the woman you love—and maybe kick some changeling ass along the way."

CHAPTER 13

*E*ven the blazing morning rays over Havenwood Falls could not permeate the darkness that hovered inside the dense patch of wood. The heavy feeling wound itself, snakelike, in lengths that ran dark acres around the areas that surrounded Noelani's well, ensnaring those that would cross its barriers in gloom as easily as a spider's victim might be caught in its web. The moment Maris and Simon entered the woods, the shadows and silence and cold descended upon them, marking passage inside a world that was simultaneously both Havenwood Falls and a place separate from it. For better or for worse, they had left the safety of the town—though Maris had to seriously question how safe a town that was home to leagues of supernatural beasties could be—and were moving steadily in the direction of where darker things lay in wait. The worst part of it all, Maris debated, was a toss-up between the fact that she was in love with the darkest of those dark things, or that the darkness was hers, an inherited curse passed down by a father she'd only barely known.

There was also the fact that if she failed, she'd take Simon down with her, and she'd be just another name lost to a bad legacy. Her father had taken his bride; she'd take someone who was very possibly her only friend.

Then again, her only friend was a *dragon*. Maybe the odds were slightly in her favor this time around.

Shaking off the shivers, Maris let the tingling in her wrist that had begun as soon as she'd crossed the forest's threshold act as a beacon, pulling her toward her fate. It insisted she veer left, toward a particularly menacing clump of trees carved out of sharp angles and shadow. Steeling her nerves, she, along with Simon, began moving in the direction Maris hoped would lead them to Noelani's well.

The movement through the forest seemed slower going today than it had last night. The sound of their footsteps was lost in the frozen hush of the wood, and cold air settled on their shoulders as they trekked deeper into the eerie darkness of the forest. Everything in the forest seemed to be reaching toward them—the spindly branches of the black trees that reached with long, skeletal fingers; the sharp, snaring bramble that clung to the bottoms of their pants and stabbed its way up their legs; even the cold, penetrating wind that sliced through their clothes and burned their skin.

Maris's body was tensed and on alert, and the silent shriek on the air seemed to swell in her ears with every thickening shadow and darkened passageway. Beside her, she could feel energy radiating off Simon that mimicked her own—waiting, uneasy, and on edge. She thought of asking Simon if he could hear the stilted scream she heard but thought better of it. Of course he could hear it. He could probably hear more than she could, and she really wasn't interested in him sharing. She didn't need anything else to add to her nightmares; they had a full cast of scary things already.

"How far did you walk last night before you got to the clearing?" Simon asked, his voice husky and hushed above her.

Maris continued to scan the darkness, torn between anticipation of finding the well and fear of seeing any movement whatsoever that would remind her they were not alone in the woods. "I'm not sure. Not long, I don't think. But I kind of lost track of things when that changeling showed itself. I just ran and sort of stumbled into it."

Simon produced an agreeable sort of noise but didn't produce judgment for her poor planning. "They're known to give a fright, that's for sure."

A harsh laugh pushed itself out of Maris's mouth. "That's an understatement. Those things were scary as hell."

"They can be."

"Does that mean there are times when those things *aren't* scary?"

Sucking in a deep breath, Simon used his arm to hold back a branch that looked like it was made out of claws so they could pass under it unmolested. "They're fae. Neutral. But can be swayed by light or dark. Once, they might have been nothing more than wood sprites, but when darkness took over this patch of wood, it covered them, too."

Great, Maris thought. *More bad juju to add to the Heilen name.*

"But we really shouldn't talk about them. Not here," Simon continued.

Maris was just about to ask why when the little hairs on the back of her neck stood on end.

"Because they'll hear you," Simon finished, as a small band of figures emerged from the depths of the shadows behind a gathering of particularly menacing sharp-leaved trees.

The changelings were figures carved out of midnight, but Maris could make out the shape of Addie's trademark glasses and the small stature of another she recognized as the diminutive stature of Jakeel. Worse, she realized as a hard knot curled in the pit of her stomach, she saw her own low ponytail on one of the shadowy figures and, on the final form, the curled ends of Simon's hair under the brim of a something pretending to be a cap. They moved silently as they filled in the blank spaces between the tall shapes of the trees, but even coated in darkness Maris could make out the jerky, unnatural movements, the strange, waxen faces.

Maris and Simon stood rooted to the ground as the band of changelings pushed silently through the wood. "I think they heard us," Maris said. "What happens if they catch us?"

"I don't know," Simon admitted, and the shock of this was enough to swivel Maris's head away from the changelings and to the man at her side.

"You don't *know*?"

He shrugged. "I could tell you what the stories say, but you wouldn't like that either. Truth is, no one has dared venture into these woods since . . . the event. They stay in, we stay out, and life goes on. Call it a truce."

The changelings were growing in number around them and had now taken on a mass so numerous that Maris found it nearly impossible to distinguish their forms from the brush around them. It was like they were coming out of the trees themselves, or that the trees were changing shape and molding into the forms of her friends in town. A hundred terrifying scenarios flashed through Maris's mind, her psyche suggesting even darker and more twisted outcomes than she would have thought herself capable of, as the band of changelings closed silently in around them, pulling and stretching the darkness with them until it felt like all the air was being frozen out of the wood and Maris worried she might lose consciousness.

Beside her, Simon had begun to radiate heat.

"There are too many," he surmised, and Maris noticed that he seemed larger, thicker somehow, as if his body were expanding. It was hard to tell in the dark, but she could sense that he was changing—no, *shifting*. A swell of panic rose in Maris's chest as suddenly she found herself in the presence of monsters: a band of changelings taking on mutated forms of people she cared about at her back, and her single friend morphing into a fire-breathing beast at her side.

"*RUN!* Find her," Simon bellowed, his voice no longer smooth and masculine but harsh and raspy—a man's voice emerging from the snout of a dragon—and, as soon as the command from her brain reached her feet, she did.

Maris ran, crashing through the only open space in the trees she could find as her tattoo burned like fire on her wrist. She sped through the darkness, the branches of the trees once more slicing at her face as she screamed Noelani's name. Why she did this, she wasn't sure, but a cursed woman who lived in rage and grief at the bottom of a well somehow seemed safer than what Maris was leaving behind.

Crashing through another dense patch of trees, Maris emerged into the silent stillness of the meadow, too dark and cast in shadow in what should have been the brightness of morning. Noelani's well was in the distance, and already Maris could see the winding tangles of her black hair creeping over the edges and slithering like snakes along stones and frozen ground toward her. Maris took one final glance back and saw the wings of a great dragon, its scales glittering even in the absence of starlight. A blast of bright light erupted as a burst of fire cut through the darkness, and the resulting scream of the changelings was so immediately terrible and horrifying that it scarred itself into Maris's heart. She stood, her mouth agape as she gawked in the direction of the forest, her mind unable to fully comprehend what she had just seen as she felt the tendrils of Noelani's hair wrap around her ankles and pull her to her knees.

It's now or never, Maris thought, watching the dark black ribbons of Noelani's hair wind themselves like coils around her legs.

Maris did not resist. She let herself be pulled toward the well, and when her feet bumped against its edges and she saw the ghostly figure of Noelani wafting underwater, she grabbed ahold of the woman's hands as she pushed herself into the water. Icy coldness stole her breath as Maris slipped with Noelani into the blackness.

CHAPTER 14

*T*he fall down the well was shorter than Maris would have imagined, not that she had given any particular thought to how long such a thing might take. Even more surprising than this, however, was the ease with which Maris found she could breathe. She'd half-expected to drown in some fathomless body of watery darkness, but she was instead sitting quite comfortably on what might have been a bed of soft moss in a large underground cavern. There was water above and beneath her, but in between existed a small plateau of dry land, the coast of an underwater lake that might have once been more beautiful than any of the places Maris had ever visited on her wanderings. Now it was as grim and haunted as everything in this part of Havenwood Falls. What's more, the feeling here was different than the forest. It wasn't frightening, not exactly, though it was certainly uninviting. The whole place was drenched in an unspeakable melancholy, so that the weight of it pressed down upon Maris, suffocating every bit of joy from her bones until—eventually—all that would remain was infinite sadness.

For the moment at least, Noelani was nowhere to be seen and Maris felt alone—utterly alone actually, which in itself was a distinctly unsettling realization. Taking a moment to return her breathing—and her pulse—to a state closer to normal, Maris sipped in stale, frozen air while her eyes adjusted to the dim. Gradually, her heartbeat slowed and her surroundings came into view. She'd expected this place to be a pitch-blackness even darker than the forest, but it wasn't—not completely. It was still dark—still almost unbearably cold—but Maris could clearly distinguish the boundaries of the new world she'd fallen into. There was no source of light that Maris could see, but nevertheless, the area around her was lit by a faintly ethereal kind of glow, gray and otherworldly, as if the place were formed from dust and ash. The only deviation from this somber setting was a mystical sort of sparkle, though even it seemed a possessed thing, the phantom light reflecting off the surfaces of the shapes around Maris as though everything was coated in a fine dusting of coarse sugar.

Using her hands to steady her, Maris pulled herself into an upright position. This dismal gray place, she saw, was an underground cavern situated at the bottom of a small waterfall, anchored in place by a shallow lake of murky gray water. Above her, Maris could see a tunnel that stretched upward toward the mouth of the well, and beyond that, Maris could make out the sky overhead, midnight blue well before noon. A fog had crept in, like a funeral shroud that eclipsed the stars, which only added to the gloom. In the space below where Maris sat, the cavern was stark and barren. Like the forest outside, what once must have been lush vegetation was frozen in various states of decay, the petals and blooms as delicate and brittle as spider webs. It was cold here—cold enough that Maris could see her breath in front of her face —but the air was stale and vaguely rancid, like a freezer left closed for too long. And it hurt to breathe too deeply, so that Maris could only draw quick shallow breaths, which only added to the feeling of despair. Even though she was standing in the open air on dry land, Maris couldn't shake the feeling that she might drown if she moved too quickly.

Reaching out to a rock, Maris rubbed some of the glittering substance onto her fingertips. She brought it to her lips and, tasting it, grimaced at the result. It wasn't sugar after all, but salt. Just like it had in her dream, salt covered every surface, glinting and gleaming at her as evidence of all the tears Noelani had cried in the decades since

Maris's father had stolen her magic away and left her with nothing but pain. The salt crusted over everything—rocks and crags, the decaying corpses of plant matter, and even the shallow pond itself all were covered, no inch left immune to Noelani's suffering.

A faint slithering sound interrupted the silence, and Maris's heartbeat resumed its frantic pace as the moss—which Maris now realized was not moss at all, but a nest of matted, dark hair—began to shift and slide beneath her feet. It moved more quickly here than it had above the well, and the nest made fast work of entrapping Maris, twisting and curling around her in a nest of tangles. Fearing that if she struggled too much against it, it might swallow her like quicksand, Maris stayed as still as she could manage, trying to ignore the sensation of what felt like snakes wrapping around her body—the strands winding tighter and tighter as Maris grew ever colder and even her shallow breaths were reduced to little more than small sips. The tattoo on her wrist was hot—iron hot—and it burned from its place on her skin, every bit as scorching and painful as if someone had held a brand to her flesh.

When a final lock of hair coiled itself around Maris's neck and the tangle had grown still, the slithering noise of its movement was interrupted by a thick gulping sound. Maris watched as, in a heave, Noelani's face was born forth above the embryotic syrup of the shallow pond. Even with her gaunt features and black, soulless eyes, her thin-shriveled lips and pallid, waterlogged flesh, Maris could still sense the beauty underneath, and it was devastating. The creature's mouth curled around the shape of Maris's name as it groaned and lurched in a macabre dance, jerking and twisting out of the water as it made its way toward her.

"*Heilen*," Noelani the rusalka called in her strange, strangled voice. "Heilen."

Much to her own surprise, Maris answered, her voice calm and soothing even under the pressure of Noelani's hair and the fire in her wrist—even despite the weight of tears in her throat.

"Come away with me," she invited Noelani, using the same phrase she had heard her love utter so often in her dreams. Maris realized at that moment that this might have been a terrible mistake, but, she decided, if she were to die in this place, at least she would do so with her true love, and so she called the wasted beauty of Noelani to her. "Come to me, Noelani."

Maris watched as Noelani made her slow, contorted journey over the banks, her lovely white dress reduced to scraps of rotted fabric that tore even as she crawled forward and pulled herself within a finger's length of where Maris waited, nearly frozen from cold and fear. Swallowing her rising panic, Maris continued to invite Noelani closer, her words eventually giving way to a single one—*come*—as Noelani's rancid, bitter breath filled Maris's nose. Maris knew she should be horrified, that she should thrash and fight with all her might, that she should scream for help and do everything in her power to flee this monster coming to claim her.

But there was no time to do any of that. Something was changing.

As the thing that had once been Noelani inched forward, the tattoo on Maris's wrist began to glow softly, the light seeping upward through the cracks in her bonds as it spread warmth throughout her body. As Noelani crept into the ring of light shining from the star on Maris's wrist, she began to undergo a slow transformation, the darkness melting away as the light shone on the image of the woman Maris had seen so many nights in her dreams. Maris knew it was a trick, some kind of projection only seen when the creature came this close and not real—or was it?

Realization hit Maris like a bolt of lightning in the deep, dark cave. This dark version of Noelani was nothing more than a curse, and this ragged, monstrous form was a disguise—a mask—intended to hide Noelani's brightness behind a wall of pain, an exaggerated version of the same dark emptiness Maris had carried within herself. The darkness had consumed Noelani, had covered her up and locked her inside a degrading shell, but it was not her true form. The naiad's spirit was still there, hidden underneath. It was desperate and unchanged and crying out for help. The dreams Maris had been having were not just lovely fantasies, nor were they simple visions of the woman fated for her. They were cries for help, Maris understood, desperate pleas for salvation. For healing. For her not just to come find her, but to come and save her. The truth of this was more than the shape of Maris's tattoo; it was clear in the light that shone from it—the healing light that proved that Maris, and perhaps Maris alone, could see Noelani for what she truly was. And, more important than this, that in Maris's light, Noelani could be as she once was, if only someone could bring her out of the darkness she was trapped in.

If Maris could find a way to free her from the dark.

Noelani was now firmly encased in Maris's light, and Maris no longer saw the creature that had crept out of the gray waters. Instead, she saw a silken veil of hair the color of strawberries, a milky complexion. Noelani's eyes were the shade of springtime grass, her lips soft petals of blooming roses. She was a beautiful and lively thing, even though ragged breath still issued forth from her lips, and Maris knew, vaguely, that anyone else watching would have seen a monster hanging over her and not this lovely creature. But Maris didn't. Maris saw only the woman whom she'd fallen in love with over many nights and many years. She saw the nights they'd spent together; the constancy—the connection that had anchored her in a life spent flailing about always searching for something she could never seem to find. And then she realized something. Maris had thought she'd never been in love before, but knew now that she had been wrong—she'd been in love with Noelani this entire time, and had only been waiting for the chance to find her way back to her. And that sort of longing love changed everything, unshackling Maris from the need to run and inspiring the desire to fight. To hold on tighter than she ever had and never let go. To force Noelani back to her in the same way that she had been begging Maris to come to her each night in every single one of her dreams.

A new strength surged in Maris. "Noelani, look at me," she demanded.

"Heilen," came the strangled word again, the voice that came from between the rose-petal lips the sound of crinkling paper.

Maris felt the coils of hair squeezing her, the pressure growing tighter and tighter until she could barely draw breath. She was drowning, she knew—drowning in the same deep, consuming void that Noelani had been trapped in for decades—and she was simultaneously both the only one with the power to stop it, and powerless to do anything to fight against it.

With the last bit of energy Maris had left, she pushed her left hand through the hair that bound her. The star was blazing white light in the dusky darkness, and Noelani's eyes darted to it as Maris pulled her hand inward so that her fingers could embrace Noelani's face. The smooth skin was hard and clammy beneath Maris's hand, but she ignored this as she pitched herself forward so that her lips were only inches away from Noelani's. The other woman struggled against her touch, her mouth opening to reveal a swallowing darkness as she shrieked.

"Heilen," Noelani screamed, the sound of her voice at once so forceful and piercing that Maris felt her eardrums vibrate with the threat of bursting.

"Come away with me," Maris used her last breath to whisper as she pressed her mouth against Noelani's thin, cracked lips. Feeling herself slipping into darkness, Maris held the kiss, held Noelani's face to hers, tasting her own name as the light issuing forth from her wrist began to flicker and fade . . .

. . . but then something changed.

A taste like honey lit on Maris's lips, and she realized that Noelani was kissing her back, her cool, smooth hands cupping her face as her kiss breathed life back into Maris, chasing away the encroach of waiting death.

Noelani's lips pulled away from hers, and Maris found that she could breathe easily again. She was warm, too, and the weight of sadness had been lifted from her shoulders so that it felt like she might float all the way upward, out of the well, and back into the world above. When she opened her eyes, the world had been recolored: the water in the pond sparkling and clear, the decaying vegetation restored to vibrant blooms—even the darkness above the well's mouth the crisp cornflower blue of mid-afternoon.

None of these could compare to Noelani herself, who was once again as lovely as she had been in Maris's dreams as she smiled down at Maris in her fully restored glory, a thing untarnished by darkness. There was an instant feeling of fullness that passed between them, an energy more full of excitement and anticipation than even the biggest of Maris's adventures. It was a dream made real, the current of an indescribable connection plucked out of a dream and into the solid reality of life, and Maris's entire body felt like it was sparkling, as if light was flushing out from her pores and she was a star made flesh.

The two women gazed lovingly into each other's eyes for the space of a few heartbeats, but it was Noelani who spoke first. "You found me," she said in a voice that was like the sound of bells. "You pulled me back from the darkness."

A blush crept into Maris's cheeks. "No," she insisted. "You found me. You've been calling me to you for as long as I can remember. I've dreamed of you every night."

She touched Noelani's cheek, marveling at her beauty, her familiarity, at the sense of wholeness Maris felt for the first time in her life. With Noelani in her arms a void inside of her had been filled, the deep craving she had tried for a lifetime to fill with scores of nameless people and places now utterly full. She had been driven to find something, someone, and she had wasted so much time looking when everything she'd ever needed had been here all along.

"I never knew it was you I was looking for." Maris smiled, drawing Noelani's face into hers. "You are my Water."

Noelani nuzzled her cheek against Maris's as their lips met. "And you, Maris Heilen, are my Star."

EPILOGUE

The next day, Addie retraced Maris's tattoo with permanent ink and made her a resident of Havenwood Falls. Maris had never counted on permanency, either on her skin or in her life, but now that she'd found Noelani—as well as new friends who had become the first family she'd ever really known—she had no intention of ever leaving. Her father's crime might have earned him banishment from the magical little town in the Colorado mountains, but it was the only place on Earth that Maris felt truly at home.

Just as her shuttle driver had promised on the evening she'd arrived in town, the tow service retrieved Maris's car from the truck stop in Grand Junction and delivered it to Whisper Falls Inn. Until plans could be made to build a more long-term structure near the well, Maris planned to split her time between the inn and Noelani's forest. She never slept in the turret again, though, preferring to spend her nights in the company of her love in the cave beneath the well, where they lay in each other's arms and stared at the stars, no longer held apart by the space of dreams. When she wasn't with Noelani, Maris tended bar at Fallview Tavern & Grille, where she and Simon continued to build their friendship, and Addie promised to help her learn more about any magic she might have inherited from what her father had stolen from Noelani's eyes. Maris was human, but her call to the water and the residue of Noelani's magic in her blood might mean there was more to Maris than met the eye.

Light had once more returned to the dark forest, the changelings that had crept into the woods had disappeared to wherever it was that changelings disappeared to, and the warm sunshine soon recolored the meadow in vibrant hues of new life. The weeds shrank and flowers bloomed, and within days, the area surrounding the well was as lovely and fragrant as ever. The cold and salt melted away, so that the meadow was warmer and brighter than before. Finally, when water once more lapped at the top of the well, Noelani's sweet voice again filled the wind of the forest with song.

For the time being, Noelani's well would remain a secret in Havenwood Falls, both to allow the naiad's magic to restore and to give the privacy that was due to her and Maris. Only Simon and Addie had visited the well, where on a particularly sunny afternoon they helped construct a small grave marker in memory of Stella Malley, the woman who had died in Noelani's well so many years before.

On Noelani's instruction, the marker was made of a white crystal, a star etched on its surface above the woman's name.

"I can't believe my father was capable of something so evil," Maris reflected, as she and Simon secured Stella's gravestone in a patch of thistle not far from the well. She traced her fingers over the star before rising to her feet, using the fabric of her jeans to wipe away the last remnants of dirt that had accompanied the burial. "I feel so ashamed of the legacy my family's name brought to this place. I don't know how to make it up."

Beside her, Simon placed his hand reassuringly on Maris's shoulder. He didn't have any words of comfort to offer, but he had none of judgment either. That was one of the things Maris liked most about Simon—that he could say so much without saying much of anything at all.

"There is darkness in all of us, Maris, my love," Noelani reminded her, a serene smile playing on the corners of her lips while she sat next to Addie on the rim of the well. "Only the darkness in some is stronger than the light. It is up to each of us to choose which side we fall on, but there must be those on both sides, I'm afraid. There is a balance that must be kept. Without the darkness, the light would never be as bright."

Addie nodded agreeably as Maris and Simon rejoined the pair at the well, the foursome settling easily on the soft grass. Maris slipped her hand inside Noelani's as the naiad leaned her head on Maris's shoulder.

"Tell that to poor Stella," Maris said with a sigh.

"Can you tell us more about Stella Malley?" Addie asked. "No one truly knows what happened that night. Maybe it would help us all to be able to move on if we knew the whole story."

It was Noelani's turn to sigh. A wistful look passed across her face, but it was gone in a blink as she turned her eyes toward Maris. "Yes, I will tell you that story one day, but not yet," she said. "For now, I need to heal, and I need to know the woman who saved me."

✦

We hope you enjoyed this story in the Havenwood Falls series featuring a variety of supernatural creatures. The series is a collaborative effort by multiple authors.

Havenwood Falls Books by Seven Jane:
Of Salt and Stars
The Drowning Bride

You might also enjoy these stories:
Forget You Not by Kristie Cook
Ink & Fire by R.K. Ryals
Toil & Trouble by Melissa Wright

Also look for the YA line, Havenwood Falls High; the historical paranormal line, Legends of Havenwood Falls; the sexier side of town, Havenwood Falls Sin & Silk; the local supernatural college, Sun & Moon Academy; and the Havenwood Falls holiday short story anthologies.

Stay up to date at www.HavenwoodFalls.com

ABOUT THE AUTHOR

Seven Jane is an author of dark fantasy and speculative fiction. Her debut novel, *The Isle of Gold*, was published by Black Spot Books in October 2018. She is represented by Gandolfo Helin & Fountain Literary Management and supported by Smith Publicity.

On Facebook, Twitter, and Instagram @sevenjanewrites or at www.sevenjane.com.

ACKNOWLEDGMENTS

Many thanks are due to Toni Miller, Lynn Shaw, and Jenny Bynum, three wonderful ladies whose eyes and insight I would not trade for anything in the world.

To Kristie Cook and the team at Ang'dora Productions, LLC, who have welcomed me into the magical world of Havenwood Falls.

ACKNOWLEDGEMENTS

AN EXCERPT

~ A Havenwood Falls New Adult Novella ~

Havenwood Falls

Redefined

USA Today Bestselling Author

MORGAN WYLIE

Redefined (A Havenwood Falls Novella) by Morgan Wylie

From *USA Today* Bestselling Author Morgan Wylie - She's a lead witch assassin—until he leads her to question everything she's ever believed.

Hollis Blackstone is a lead assassin for her father's rogue band of witch hunters. For longer than she can remember, her father, Dante, has had two missions: rid the world of witches and locate his estranged family kept from him by his sister's rebellion. Working off a lead, Hollis finds her way through the mysterious borders of Havenwood Falls. Her father's orders were to gather intel on the whereabouts of all the Blackstones, all the witches, and the seat of their power. But then she meets the irresistible Ryne Calloway.

Half witch and half phoenix, Ryne hasn't been in Havenwood Falls for long. Rejected by his father's clan because of his witch heritage, he knows all about suppressing who he really is. In town for a fresh start, he hopes to relax and have fun. And that's exactly what he plans to do with the pretty new girl who strolled into town with a stick up her butt.

Ryne opens Hollis's eyes, widening her perspective beyond the hatred she's been taught. But when her father seeks her out, everything begins to unravel. She's finally found someone who loves her for her, but she's about to lose him before ever having the chance to love him back.

REDEFINED

BY MORGAN WYLIE

Hollis Blackstone stared at herself in her bedroom mirror, seeing only the assassin she had been created to be, wondering if there was anything else she might ever become. She had quickly gained the position as one of the lead assassins for her father, Dante Blackstone. Being a witch hunter was more than her job; it was her entire life, day and night. Hollis had been training to be the best since she could remember. On nights when the teams ransacked home after home, she caught a rare glimpse of him smiling at her—at what she'd accomplished—and she believed him to be proud of her. The teams liked to make a mess of each witch's home they attacked, but Hollis preferred her team to be stealthy, more deadly. The lack of interruption to one's home seemed to send a greater message than a tantrum of violent proportions.

Her room was nothing more than an empty shell, a cavern of unrealized possibilities. Hollis didn't waste time decorating her rooms, for there would always be another, in another town. Her father's organization—her family—moved around more often than they stayed in one place, or so it seemed the past year or so. Plus it was just one more thing to have to worry about, to take her focus away from her job—her obsession.

Pulling on her black leather jacket, despite the early May warm weather, she covered the multiple tattoos on her shoulders stretching down toward her elbows. Hollis fluffed her long dark hair in the mirror, checking to ensure the scar at her hairline was hidden, and made sure she was presentable. She had been called in to see her father, and he didn't tolerate sloppiness or tardiness. Dante always dressed impeccably to impress and to intimidate, and he expected nothing less from his teams. An inept capability to be present when requested was unacceptable to Dante.

They had only recently set up this home, and Hollis didn't even remember what city they were in this time, but she knew they were somewhere near Santa Fe, New Mexico. Dear old dad had been chasing a lead in his lifelong obsession to track down the other Blackstones—those he considered lost and in need of his guidance— and the secret place in which they lived. About a year and a half ago, they had almost found it, but somehow it mysteriously—most likely magically—slipped through their fingers, and they couldn't remember anything about where they had been or where they were trying to get. Her father had been infuriated.

He had been on a rampage ever since they had let Macy Blackstone— who'd been staying with them—get away. Macy had been the biggest lead they'd had in a long time. Her father received slight pulls in the right direction, which he could never describe other than to say he "sensed the spirit of his sister Marie and the rest of his family who *should* be with him." At other times, Dante would utter vague accounts of being so close to the name of the town in his mind only to have it slip away like a lost memory he tried to force to the surface. Somehow they still mysteriously received secret letters from Aunt Letti to Grace and the other old gals no matter where they were, but her teams could never trace the letters' origins.

Hollis strode down the hall with purpose and ownership, stopping only when she arrived at her dad's office. Knocking twice, she didn't wait long. He was straight to business as he called through the door.

"Come in, daughter mine," Dante called through the door, his voice strong and sure. It could have been one of several of the Blackstones who lived with them at the door, but he seemed to always know when Hollis was near. Dante had lived a long time and been quite prolific with reproduction over the span. Even Grace, who appeared to be in her seventies and was half hunter and half human, was one of his descendants. Hollis refused to consider them all siblings since the ages varied so drastically, but they were family just the same. Right as Hollis turned the handle, a young girl in her early teen years with golden blond hair skipped around the corner.

"Have fun, Hollis!" Sunny called with a singsong voice and a big smile.

Hollis didn't let anyone close, but if anyone could get under her skin and attach themselves to her, it was Sunny. Sunny had a way about her that would disarm the most hardened criminal. The family referred to her as their "little ray of caffeinated sunshine." Hollis reached out and tugged on one of Sunny's pigtails.

"Thanks, kid. See ya 'round."

"Maybe, maybe not," she continued in her singsong tone and shrugged. Sunny suddenly stopped and then frowned. Her expression sobered, then she stared into Hollis's eyes. "I'll miss you, but I'm happy for you." Sunny came in for a quick, unexpected hug, then turned without another word. She skipped down the hallway, leaving Hollis with a dumbfounded look on her face.

"What was that about?" Hollis wondered under her breath.

"Are you coming in, Hollis?" Dante asked with an edge in his voice. He didn't like to be kept waiting.

"Sorry, Father. Sunny stopped me," she offered as an excuse, the only excuse she would ever use, and the only one he would allow. He gave her a sharp nod.

"Come sit. I'm waiting on Nala and Rachel. And here they are now."

Hollis turned to find the two other hunters walk through the door. They sauntered in, their heads high and chins jutted out, proud to have been summoned. They were both exceptional hunters in their own rights, but Hollis was better. Their presence caused her to wonder why he wanted to see all three of them. Perhaps he had another mission for them, though they had each been out on a witch hunt last night.

"Take your seats," Dante directed as he stood, straightening his suit and refastening the bottom button. In his suits, he appeared dapper and put together like Pierce Brosnan in a James Bond movie, even down to the silver streaking his otherwise black sideburns. "It has recently come to my attention through a reliable source—"

"You mean snitch," Rachel sarcastically snickered.

Dante inclined his head. "Such a crass term. I prefer 'source.' Anyway, this source confirmed what a separate source had previously supplied. The town we have been looking for is, in fact, in Colorado. It is called Havenwood Falls."

"Weren't we just in Colorado, like a year ago?" Nala impatiently asked. She had been one of the main hunters first tailing, then keeping watch, on Macy Blackstone when she had inadvertently stumbled upon them.

"Indeed, but my memory of it has remained maddeningly elusive. No doubt a side effect of those damned witches the *other* Blackstones associate with."

"They shouldn't be allowed to use the name Blackstone," Rachel spat with disgust. Nala and Hollis both agreed.

"No, no. They are of our blood. Though they are misguided, we can bring them back into the fold, into our family, and redirect their purpose—help them see the error of their ways, so to speak," Dante clarified, looking each girl in the eye to ensure they understood.

"Do you know where in Colorado?" Hollis cut to the chase.

"No. That is the frustrating part. However, we know it is somewhere in the middle of the state. Most likely somewhere with a significant area of land where they could hide an entire town."

"How do we know your 'sources' aren't sending us on a wild goose chase?" Nala asked as she whipped her long blond hair behind her shoulder.

Dante sneered, and an evil glint entered his eyes. "I extracted the information from the witch myself. She couldn't help but tell me."

Nala and Rachel each swallowed hard. They knew what kind of

methods the source would have had to endure for Dante to get the information he wanted. Hollis didn't flinch. She knew he did what he had to, to get what he needed.

"Well, it's about damn time. When do we go?" Rachel asked, readjusting in her seat as if she wasn't afraid of Dante's tactics. They all feared him. The ones like Hollis had the ability to hide their fear, which separated them from the others.

"No." Dante surveyed the girls slowly, taking measure of something they weren't aware of. "For this mission, I need to be able to completely trust the person I send. She would have to be able to go undercover, be skilled at listening, and have the ability to not act on instinct—to conceal her hunter side for the greater good. For this mission, I choose Hollis. She is the best suited."

Without reaction, Hollis simply nodded her acceptance. The other girls groaned.

"Then why are we here?" Rachel asked. She had a tendency to speak out of turn. Dante put up with it to a point. He had reached that point. The look he gave her had her shrinking back into her seat. Hollis couldn't help the glow of approval she kept hidden in her chest. Rachel got on her nerves the most.

"*That* is exactly why I chose her. Hollis can control her reactions and simply observe. Also, not to mention, Macy has seen you both and most likely would recognize you right away. She never met Hollis during her stay, as Hollis was out on an extended mission." Hollis realized he had called the other girls in to teach them a lesson and to, once more, instill competition amongst them by elevating one over the other. She didn't agree with his tactics for camaraderie amongst teams, but he did get results. He turned and looked to her. "Will you go, daughter?"

"Of course, Father. When should I be ready to leave for Colorado?"

"Tomorrow morning. I will have Grace get flights prepared. Pack light. Disguise yourself. I want you to blend in. Be a tourist, if need be. I want specific information on the town and certain people within it. I'll get a list together while you pack."

Hollis inclined her head in a half nod and half bow, ready to serve.

"How are you so sure she'll find it based on 'somewhere in the middle of Colorado'?" Nala asked, but Hollis could hear the tinge of jealousy behind her tone.

"Can you find it, Hollis?" Dante pointedly asked.

"I won't come home until I do."

Dante smiled. "That's my girl."

And that was how Hollis found herself at the private airport in Grand Junction, waiting for a shuttle to take her to Montrose, yet another small city in the middle of the Colorado mountains.

Purchase *Redefined* where books are sold.

www.ingramcontent.com/pod-product-compliance
Lightning Source LLC
Chambersburg PA
CBHW052003170626
46808CB00007B/2762